Virtue at Market Price

Being a true account of the adventures of
E. Pluribus Van Slyke, Lt. (jg), Ret., in
the taming of the pirate menace and the
securing of American womanhood.

As recorded by

E. Pluribus Van Slyke

in a world orchestrated by

M.E. Meegs

The Oeuvre of M.E. Meegs

Empyreal Privateer

Virtue at Market Price

Them Shes Be Pirates

No Time for Fish Tales

Hush, My Inner Sleuth

LycophosPress.com

The Byblos Foretold Novaplex

All's Fair, Mrs. Biddle

Babes at Sea

Peddlers All

Dames Engaged

The Fly Maiden's Book of Virtues

The Circensiad

ByblosForetold.com

Virtue at Market Price

M.E. Meegs

&

E. Pluribus Van Slyke

Lycophos Press

Northampton, Mass.

First Print Edition 2018

Lycophos Press
Northampton, Mass.

ISBN: 978-1-938710-34-6

To fickle Mnemosyne and her inciting daughters

CHAPTER 1.

SNATCHED AT SEA!

I could tell at once from the ugly look the bond broker gave me that I'd overplayed my hand. He sat just opposite, his malevolent mien mixing equal parts indignation and satisfaction: indignation at having been plucked, and satisfaction at having at last detected it. We were playing draw and I'd discarded two duds. When the dealer tossed me my replacements, I palmed a knave and replaced it with the queen of diamonds I'd held from the last hand. That gave me a sister pair with an ace high.

"Get up!" The wily jobber had come prepared. He produced a little revolver from an inside pocket and pointed it in the direction of my now palpitating heart. "He's got a sixth card on him somewhere."

By then it was stuffed deep between the seat cushions of the chair I'd only just vacated. But they were a thorough bunch. After having me undress, they tore apart a rather expensive suit. (On that point, at least, I was in luck—unlike the Parisian tailor still awaiting payment.) Then, in a matter of seconds, they dismantled what had seemed a quite solid piece of furniture. When the Texas cattle baron located the jack hiding amongst the upholstery, he announced the fact by calling for a rope.

Egotist that I am, I'd always harbored the expectation that I'd someday achieve some level of notoriety. But being the first man lynched aboard a steamship of the French Line wasn't exactly what I'd had in mind. Fortunately, the wiser heads among the mob countered with a proposal to call the purser. Not so fortunately, they were quickly overruled by heads of even more colorful imagination than that of the Texan.

The debate turned now on a choice between two forms of punishment deemed more in keeping with the sea-voyage theme: keelhauling, or walking the plank. It was a lopsided vote. The fault lay with an English coal magnate who took a good deal of relish in explaining what exactly keelhauling entailed.

"A rope is brought under the beam of the ship. The victim's tied to it and then drawn under the boat. There his body's bashed against the hull by the swells, and then nearly torn in half crossing the keel! If he survives, he's given another chance."

"Gets let off?"

"No. *Gets another chance to die!* He's sent down the opposite way, then back and forth until all that's left tied to the rope is a pair of bloody arms!"

Cheers all around. Well, nearly so. For once in my life, I was struck dumb. By the time I'd prepared my rebuttal, my wrists had been bound with a length of cord and a napkin stuffed in my mouth.

Once we were out on deck—me in my union suit and nothing else—the logistical obstacles to their plan became readily apparent. The S.S. *Paris* was a modern luxury liner and the distance between the boat deck and the keel considerable. They'd already tied one end of a coil of rope to my ankle, but it was hardly likely to be long enough. And then came the not insignificant problem of how to get the rope under the keel in the first place. The coal magnate admitted his ignorance on this point.

So the plank it was. Aided by the light of a full moon, they located a gangway stowed among the air vents and dragged it out to between the davits of two of the lifeboats. It ran about twenty feet and they gradually slid one end out over the sea. When it began to tilt, three of the party's heavier members got on to act as counter-weights.

It seemed to me the joke had been taken far enough, so I spat out the gag. "I should have you know, protests will be made."

"Not by you, they won't." Again, cheers all around.

"My wife, then."

"Sounded to me like she'd be glad to be rid of you."

That from the young scion of an oil fortune who'd sat with us at dinner that evening. Sesbania had been feeling a little peevish, and partly to annoy me, and partly for her own amusement, she'd flirted with the unctuous little Lothario shamelessly. I tried another tack.

"I am an officer of the United States Navy, retired. A graduate of Annapolis. If only someone here knew me, you'd learn what a serious mistake you're making...."

Once more I'd overplayed my hand. There was, un-fortunately, someone there who knew me. Another Annapolis man who'd served in the same command during the war.

"I can tell you all you need to know about him: Van Slyke is his name. *E. Pluribus* Van Slyke."

When you've been saddled with a name like mine, you get used to hearing it spoken through a sneer. But this would-be admiral's mate took it a little far. Dirk Gilbert had been a year behind me at school and now, from the looks of it, was a genuine two-stripe lieutenant. He hadn't even been near the game table, so I couldn't imagine what interest he had in the affair.

"He was an officer, all right. And a graduate of the

Academy. But a couple years back the Navy drummed him out for gross negligence while in command."

That's the thanks I get for hardly tormenting him at all during his plebe year. He must have had in mind that embarrassing episode with the Academy mascot. You might not believe a goat capable of such things, but there's photographic evidence to the contrary.

"Not so," I protested. "My discharge was an honorable one." And it was, at least ostensibly. It's amazing what a little extortion can achieve.

"Who gives a damn about his war service?" the cattle baron inquired. Apparently, no one beside myself. "He's a card cheat, and that's all we need to know!"

They prodded me with oars taken from the boats, compelling me ever further out onto the plank. If I could just delay things long enough, one of the ship's officers would be by on his rounds and put a stop to their fun. I picked the feeblest-looking of the prodders—an old codger with a sunken chest—and launched myself headfirst at his midsection. Like hitting a brick wall. And now I'd really annoyed them. They took turns cleaning their boots on me, until finally the cattle baron righted me by means of my hair. The prodding now came not nearly so gentle as the first round.

It was mid-April, and a cool night out on the Atlantic. What's more, the ship was making over twenty knots into a steady breeze, and my underwear had been torn to shreds by the evening's trials. Goosebumps were rising on my poorly clad extremities. If we'd made it as far west as the Gulf Stream, the water might actually be warm enough to offer some relief from the chill—fleeting though it would be. I'd always been an able swimmer, but staying afloat in ocean swells with one's wrists tied would prove a pretty tall order. I began working the cord—this being the S.S. *Paris*, it was silk, and fairly slippery. But I needed time.

"I'll have you know, I'm an acquaintance of the president." This too was true. Silent Cal and I once resided in the same burg, back when he practiced peanut politics in the provinces.

"I wouldn't believe a word of that," Gilbert told them.

"I don't give a damn if you're *acquainted* with Christ *himself*," the bond broker informed me. "Tonight your appointment is with Old Nick! Into the fiery pits of hell with you!"

While his scenario would certainly offer relief from the chill, after careful analysis, I found it not to my liking. I continued working the cord about my wrists.

"Watch it! He's getting loose!"

The old codger gave me a couple energetic prods to the kidneys and I involuntarily lurched forward, just inches from the end....

Then, quite suddenly, the moon went into eclipse. A distinctive noise could be heard above that of the waves breaking on the ship's hull—like the chugga-chugga of a slowing locomotive. I looked up and was amazed to see the black mass of a giant airship! Almost as large as the liner itself, and matching its speed and course.

As all eyes fixed upon the alien vessel, three dozen ropes unfurled from the unusually large gondola. Shortly after, three dozen boarders repelled down to the boat deck. They were near enough to see in the marker lights. And believe you me, they were a decidedly scruffy gang of characters. Every man came armed: little daggers mostly, but a smattering of cutlasses as well.

The commotion drew other revelers out from the

lounge and several of the bandits began moving about the crowd, taking everything of value—wallets, watches, jewelry, etc. Very few objected. And none for long. It's remarkable how compliant even the most imperious snob becomes when he feels cold steel against his throat.

My erstwhile tormentors were, needless to say, thoroughly distracted. I had almost freed my wrists by then and began inching my way back toward the deck. Unfortunately, one of the three men acting as counterweights chose that very moment to drift off. The gangway dipped. That, in turn, alerted numbers two and three to the precariousness of their situation. They leapt off in unison, sending the gangway overboard and your terrified hero into a free fall.

As you may remember, they'd earlier tied my ankle to a long coil of rope, and I don't doubt it would have reached the brine below if it hadn't gotten entangled in something. I found myself hanging by said ankle just off the promenade deck. There were several passengers not far away and I called to them for help. But their attention was riveted by goings-on elsewhere.

A blanket atop a deck chair was moving in a manner one couldn't help but find suggestive. There were other telltale signs of occupancy as well: three stockinged feet extending from beneath the blanket, and a female voice emitting sounds reminiscent of those little red squirrels that inhabit the New England forest. The lady seemed to be pleased with how things were progressing, and either unaware of, or unconcerned with, the spectators held enthralled by her performance.

Complicating matters further, in the opposite direction were the open windows of the music room. A concert of operatic excerpts was being performed. Gruesome stuff, as you can well imagine, and loud—too loud for my shouts to overcome.

Sesbania was in there, as were most of the women traveling in first-class berths. The music room served as a sort of seraglio on the liners: one of the few places a woman could go and be sure of avoiding the company of men—well, outside the occasional eunuch.

I'd given up shouting for the moment, waiting for a lull in either the din from the music room or the squeals from the deck chair, when a couple dozen of the boarding party appeared on the scene. They barged in on the performance (operatic, not coital) and turned up the lights. While half of them displayed armaments, the other half went about the room and picked out what they seemed to consider worthy booty—jewelry, furs, etc. This prompted a good deal of excitement among the assembly. There were shrieks aplenty, and more than a few swoons. Especially once the et cetera came to include certain of the younger women.

They took only the choicest of the lot, with their taste running toward mine. A point borne out most vividly when I saw Sesbania among the captives. I was concerned, of course, but now did not seem the time to call attention to myself. As quietly as possible, I finished working my wrists free. Then, through herculean effort, I folded my body and grabbed onto the rope. An extraordinary feat, no doubt about it. But I was a man driven. My woman, my helpmate, my boon companion, etc., had been taken hostage! I feel no shame admitting I'd grown rather fond of the old girl—not to mention the bundle of assorted currencies hidden amongst her undergarments. I estimated its value at not less than fifteen thousand dollars American. Hers, of course, was without measure—though admittedly, neither was it so easily convertible.

It was slow going, inching my way up, but I managed to regain the boat deck just as the press-gang emerged from below. I waded into the crowd. When I'd sidled close enough to see Sesbania—held tight in the clutches of her abductor—our eyes met. She gave me the most curious expression—a sort of flat smile, with eyebrows raised. Then she made a little shrug, as if to say, "What can I do about it?"

"They have my daughter! Lizzie!" the bond jobber bellowed. He lunged forward, brandishing his pistol—then dropped the weapon when a dagger struck his arm. A remarkable bit of knife work—unless it was his heart the marauder aimed for.

By then a squad of crewmen with rifles appeared under the command of the first mate. They knelt, preparing to fire. But when the pirates held blades to their captives' necks, the mate had no choice but to order his men to stand down.

As if the scene weren't strange enough, suddenly a steam organ, like the calliope of a circus, took up a familiar tune. *Stairway to Paradise*, I think it was. Now each of the boarders placed a foot in a loop at the end of his respective rope and, one after another, they were winched back up—their captives hanging on for dear life.

Next came a loud whoosh, and a huge cloud emerged from the dirigible. When it had dissipated, the moon shone upon us once again.

II

There were a lot of mutterings from the crowd peopling the boat deck, now supplemented by those of the concert attendees not deemed worthy of abduction. A lot of "My Gods," et several "Nom de Dieus," und a smattering of "Mein Gotts." And an irate gentleman screaming at the first mate something about knowing a director of the Line.

A bizarre episode, no matter what your religion. And not one without cost to yours truly. But I prefer to always look on the bright side, and the bright side here was that no one would likely remember what happened at the card table half an hour before an airship of cutlass-toting pirates descended from the sky and made off with the wives and daughters of the rich and powerful. (Apart from the occasional fakes, like Sesbania and myself, they were the only sort who could afford to travel first class on a ship like the S.S. *Paris*.)

Even more providentially, I now found myself in a privileged—and not at all familiar—position: that of informed authority.

"A Zeppelin, wouldn't you say?" Gilbert asked me.

"The right size, and rigid construction, certainly. But the engines... much too loud."

You see, I was a veteran of the nascent airship branch of the Navy. During the war, after an unavoidable mishap while serving aboard a torpedo boat patrolling New York Harbor, I was dispatched to the balloon corps, keeping watch for Zeppelins over Long Island. Thankfully, the Zeppelins never made it that far.

After the war, motorized blimps—essentially bags of gas with no skeletal structure—became the new thing and I was given command of one. It was during that tour that my final mishap occurred. Actually, I should say mishaps. The first came about during war games, when I mistook the encampment of the Sells-Foto Circus for that of the opposing force. A most embarrassing episode, as you can imagine. Though not wholly without interest from a military standpoint. I think I can say without fear of contradiction that had the Romans employed motorized blimps in their confrontation with Hannibal, they would have prevailed at Cannae and saved themselves a good deal of trouble later. According to newspaper reports, it took the circus several weeks to round up its elephants.

The second mishap involved a rendezvous I'd scheduled with a certain senior officer's daughter. She'd given me faulty coordinates. Whether by accident or intentionally, I couldn't say—she was the playful sort of vixen. I ended up in bed with her stepmother. And she kept me there 'til well past dawn. The woman was insatiable. And her husband, the admiral, distinctly disagreeable. But enough reminiscing....

The bond jobber—James Rutledge was his name—had heard Gilbert and me talking and insisted we go with him to the ship's captain. But first things first. While he had his bleeding arm attended to by the doctor, I went off to augment my less than adequate attire. After dressing, I made a quick search of the cabin. I hoped Sesbania might have left a few dollars behind. But sadly, when it comes to money, she's a very meticulous girl. Two ha'pennies and half a dozen lira were the extent of it.

We found the captain already under siege by irate parents and husbands. He didn't have much to say beyond condolences and that the "proper authorities" would be alerted, and nothing at all to say in English. Who exactly the proper authorities were in this situation he left an open question.

"This is a waste of time!" Rutledge announced, then ordained that Gilbert and I accompany him to his cabin.

He had a lavish suite—I didn't even know they came

that large—and started the brandy flowing as soon as we sat down.

"I take it you have some experience with these things," he said to me. "Airships, I mean."

"Well, one doesn't like to boast. But my career in the air has been... well noted."

Gilbert let loose a little guffaw, but the old man just gave him an unfriendly look. Then he turned back to me.

"But have you ever heard of anything like this? A rogue airship, preying on a liner?"

"Frankly, no."

"I think I might have a theory," Gilbert interjected. "Unemployed Zeppelin crews. Angry at losing the war, and their station, they take up one of their old ships and seek revenge."

"But the war ended over five years ago!" the bond trader shouted. "Where were they hiding this Zeppelin?"

"Not Friedrichshafen," I replied. "The Navy sent me to the Zeppelin factory after Versailles, as part of the crew to take possession of an airship we were to be given as reparation. But the Germans insisted they'd already destroyed them all. To make sure, we went through the records with a fine-tooth comb. They were all accounted for."

Again, largely true. But it was others who did the combing of records. Meanwhile, I made a study of the steamboat that traversed the Bodensee, and, more thoroughly, of a Swiss strumpet named Eva who ran a sort of hostel on the far shore in Romanshorn.

"Besides," Rutledge added, "didn't the Zeppelins use engines running on petroleum?"

"What else would they use?" Gilbert asked.

"Steam! Didn't you hear them? And that cloud it

ejected as it left—just like a locomotive leaving the station."

The lieutenant would have none of it. "What would be the point? All the added weight of a boiler—why, it would only increase the lift required."

"The steam itself could provide the lift! Steam's lighter than air, or it wouldn't rise."

"Use steam for lift? That's preposterous! Steam is only lighter than air until it condenses, then it would drop like a stone. Isn't that so, Van Slyke?" Gilbert asked.

"Well, certainly out of the ordinary...."

"What do you mean, out of the ordinary? You know as well as I do the whole idea is patently absurd!"

He was right, of course, but I thought it wise to stay on the bond jobber's side—at least as long as the brandy held out. "There would be some obstacles to overcome. But depending on the circumstances..."

"*Depending on the circumstances?* What circumstances? A suspension of the laws of physics? A steam-powered airship is, *quite literally,* inconceivable!" By now, the lieutenant had turned as red as a beet. He took a moment to compose himself, then turned to our host. "Oh, I haven't time for this twaddle. Look, Rutledge, I am going to my cabin to write up a report. If I were you, I wouldn't give much credence to anything this man might tell you."

With that, he left us.

"It's narrow thinking like his that drove me out of the Navy," I confided. "Can't believe what he sees before his eyes if it doesn't conform to the preconceived notions he's been spoon-fed."

"Yes, I know the type.... So you think it was a steam craft too?"

"Well, of some sort. Possibly something quite beyond what we might imagine possible."

I was talking through my hat now, but the decanter was still half full. If he wanted the airship to be steam-powered, it cost me nothing to agree.

"What about the pirates themselves?"

"Difficult to say. They never said a word, all hand gestures. Certainly a well-trained and disciplined lot."

"Seemed smaller than your average Yankee. Dagos, maybe. But they kept their faces covered."

"Hard to tell. It might be they recruited a modest-sized crew to reduce load."

"Yes, that would make sense. ...I hate to think what they have in mind for my girl."

"And mine...."

"Your wife was among them?"

"Yes. God, how I miss her already." And I wasn't speaking solely of her undergarments.

I should note, perhaps, Sesbania and I were not, strictly speaking, married. Our partnership fell more along the lines of a business arrangement. People gener-ally find it easier to trust a man traveling with his wife—and vice versa.

That's not to say there was nothing else between us, but simply that things remained at the provisional stage. No claims could be made. If I went off one afternoon, I need share nothing beyond her half of any profits. Like-wise, if she were to disappear from our Monte Carlo hotel and return two full days later, exhausted, and bereft of funds, I must accept her rather flimsy excuse that a promising operation involving a scandalously wealthy widow had gone awry—as if that could explain the torn gown and the faint scent of cologne.

"Stop torturing yourself," Rutledge instructed me

needlessly. "We can't afford to waste any time on tears. We have to get to the bottom of this fast. Before..."

"Yes. Before the unthinkable...."

We had another round of brandy to console ourselves.

In truth, the worst was not the least bit unthinkable. If Sesbania got to a bank without me in tow, the loot would quite certainly be deposited in an account known only to her.

III

The next morning, I took charge of the investigation, ex officio. Both the captain and Gilbert seemed all too glad to hand off the responsibility—no doubt lining me up as ex officio scapegoat.

I began by interviewing witnesses, hoping someone might have seen or heard something that could shed some light on the affair.

"Those daggers, they were curved, and the blades were etched. Filigreed."

"Definitely from the Levant," someone chimed in. "Possibly of Ottoman origin."

"Allies of the Germans... Would seem to support my explanation," Gilbert said. "Down-on-their-luck veterans of the Kaiser's war machine."

"Perhaps," I conceded. "But also procurable at any antique shop worth its salt."

"They wore a lot of jewelry," someone pointed out. "Wasn't an ear or a finger without a ring of some sort."

"Well, they *were* pirates, after all."

"But did you notice the way they moved?" a gray-haired biddy asked no one in particular.

"Ran like girls," a boy of ten or so replied.

"No—not *ran*," the old lady corrected. "Sort of... glided."

"Yes," a comely redhead agreed. "It reminded me of a play we saw performed in Tokyo."

"Noh," her husband said.

"What do you mean, no?" She didn't look quite so comely now. "*I tell you...*"

"No, what I mean is, the Japanese theatre. It's called Noh. N-O-H."

"Oh, yes," she said. But I could tell by the set of her jaw it wasn't a heartfelt concession. She felt humiliated, and in her eyes, *he* was responsible. Steer clear of red-heads, that's my advice.

There was more of this sort of thing, observations of the pirates' dress—colorful, but not of any particular style—and their manner—determined, but not gratui-tously coarse (nearly all the women commenting on the fact that not a single buccaneer had spat the whole time they were aboard).

While dining in his cabin that evening, Rutledge and I went over the witnesses' reports. By the time the cigars were meted out, he'd concluded the pirate ship had been manned by Japanese—Orientals ranking as low in his book as the southern Europeans he'd singled out the night before.

"The Yellow Peril!" he spat through his stogie. "It was always only a matter of time!"

I kept my remarks to a minimum, brief and non-committal, and chose not to point out the contradictory evidence: the Ottoman daggers, and that the assault took place in the middle of the Atlantic, half a world away from Japan. Or the fact that the Japanese had not, to my knowledge, evinced much interest in airships.

I would need him, or his pull at least, if I was to re-cover Sesbania and her undergarments. And nothing would be lost by letting him consider himself the captain of our endeavor. I'd been playing fatheads like him since I'd convinced the Reverend Snowden I was only late for Sunday service because I'd seen his favorite mare at large and had trouble roping it.

But the effective handler must parcel out his defer-ence judiciously. Men like Rutledge expect compliance, but won't respect toadies. You must precede your acqui-escence with a certain reluctance, as if you came to agree with him only after careful consideration. Just never forget: the conclusion is preordained.

The investigation continued the next day, our last at sea, and only then did someone produce any hard evi-dence—a multicolored silk handkerchief.

"As you can see, or I should say, smell, it bears a dis-tinctive scent," the Englishman said. He was about my age, not much over thirty, and impeccably dressed. I'd wager his tailor had even been paid. "An abductor held it to the face of one of the captives."

"They all had them," a woman added.

"Ether?" Gilbert asked.

"No. Not ether." The Englishman handed him the handkerchief.

"Perfume," Gilbert announced, then handed the thing to me.

I recognized the scent immediately.

"Why didn't you come forward with this yesterday?" Gilbert asked.

I also knew the answer to that.

"Well," the fellow said rather sheepishly, "it was my

wife who recovered it. It... it appealed to her... and it wasn't until this morning..."

"You can go," I told him.

I knew, as well as he did, there'd be no easy way of explaining that scent. Or the power it held over women. *Deux nuits d'excès,* it was called: two nights of excess. And according to Sesbania, it meant just what it said. She wore a thin chain about her neck, and hanging from it was a tiny glass vial. It held no more than a few drops of this very solution. She told me she was saving it for her wedding night. If ever I suggested we try it before then, she became animated—once holding a very sharp letter opener to my throat until I swore never to touch it.

I've never taken oaths too seriously, and certainly not those demanded at knifepoint. One night, following a long evening of hard work and revelry (which, in our business, usually go hand in hand), I awoke to find her in a deep sleep. The little vial, still chained about her neck, was resting on her pillow. With all the care I could muster, I began to unscrew the top. With it nearly off, she stirred. I quickly tightened it and feigned sleep.

Not a drop had spilt. Nevertheless, she awoke in a mood best described as purposeful. I'll never forget that look in her eye, or those exhilarating hours that followed.

Later, when she became more herself, she assayed her vial, then brought her letter opener once more to my throat. She suspected. I renewed my pledge, but this time she took the precaution of placing a wax seal on the vial's top. Then she offered me her own pledge.

"If anyone but me breaks that seal, it's *you* who will be singing falsetto."

A decidedly unpleasant threat—yet one you can be very sure she meant to deliver on.

Anyway, that is how I became acquainted with the perfume. And why the Englishman could only now turn in the handkerchief, two days after his wife had taken possession of it: she'd only just finished with him.

But I kept this information to myself. It's not the sort of thing easily explained in mixed company. And I didn't see any reason to send the other loved ones into a panic. There was no telling what acts their womenfolk could be induced to perform under the influence of this, the most potent of all female aphrodisiacs (at least those of my acquaintance, and God knows I've tried just about all of them).

Fortunately for me—and Sesbania, of course—she probably had partial immunity to the stuff. Her two nights would likely be measurably less excessive than otherwise. And I felt hopeful that, given the diminutive size and almost genteel disposition of the pirates, she might very well fend off any attacks, either on her virtue or her currency-laden undergarments.

These thoughts, in turn, brought to mind her queer response to her kidnapping—the blithe shrug of the shoulders. Such sangfroid, even for so sporting a girl as she, was not what one would expect given her predicament. Come to think of it, there was a decided lack of emotion on the part of all the captives. Back in Europe, we'd viewed several depictions of the Sabine women in similar circumstances, and let me tell you, those ladies put up quite a fuss.

The perfume's calming effect may have been partly responsible. But I realized now it was something more than that. You see, they *did* run like girls, just as that kid had said. It may well be true that members of certain Japanese theatre troupes move similarly, but there are far more girls in the world than there are Japanese players.

Nonetheless, I decided I'd best keep my supposition to myself for the time being. If I turned out wrong, I'd be thought a fool. Likewise my far more fantastic supposition about the airship's propulsion. To my ears, like those of Rutledge, it *did* sound as if it were powered by steam pistons. And the whoosh *was* just like that of a locomotive. And lastly, the cloud left in its wake dissipated *exactly how a cloud of steam does.*

Gilbert was right, of course—the whole idea of a steam-powered airship is patently absurd. And, to any normal mind, quite literally inconceivable. But not, I'm afraid, *literarily* inconceivable. Especially when the novelistic mind doing the conceiving is anything but normal—though few, I imagine, are.

I realize you may feel I've gone over the top with this last hypothesis. A mere flight of fancy, you're probably thinking. But remember, I know as I write how this thing comes out. And I would hardly be likely to introduce the idea for no reason save to make myself look ridiculous. Enough said for the present. But prepare yourself.

Just after noon, we docked in New York. As we were being herded toward the gangway, I found myself just behind the ornery redhead who'd broached the comparison to the Japanese theatre. The colorful handkerchief was still about my person, and though it remained amply scented, I doubted it would remain so until I had a chance to make use of it. In a sudden burst of magnanimity, I slipped the handkerchief into the pocket of the redhead's jacket. In two days' time, I imagine her regard for her husband might have improved some—assuming he survived the interval. She looked the sort to work a man hard at whatever project she'd assigned him.

CHAPTER 2.

OF SHEBAS & PEDAGOGY

I now began to reap the returns on all my bowing and scraping. Rutledge insisted I be his guest at his Riverside Drive mansion. After the perfunctory demur, I accepted. My second option would have been a Bowery flophouse. Assuming I could find one that accepted payment in lira.

His daughter's teary-eyed fiancé sat waiting in a cab just outside the customs shed. Noyes Congdon, he was called, and a more besotted creature I hope never to meet. He droned on and on about his "poor Lizzie" until I was ready to relieve his suffering via a sharp blow to the back of the head. At first, I assumed it was fear of losing out on her father's money that motivated his concern for the girl. But intelligence soon emerged suggesting *his* fortune the more sizable of the two. And he being an orphan—likewise disclosed during his blubbering lament—the money was his to do with as he pleased. He didn't seem quite so repellent now. In judging others, I often say, one should keep an open mind until the relevant facts are revealed.

The newspapers were full of lurid accounts of the abduction. Pirates always make for good copy, but throw in a trove of bonny booty and you can't print the rags fast enough. My favorite take on it had the headline "White Slavers Meet the Newport Set." It ran in the *New York World* and carried the byline of one Aggie Ready. She led with the notion that arranging matches of mixed doubles might be more difficult than normal for the Four Hundred.

And how's the society matron to avoid a gender-skewed table of dinner guests? I suggest allowing the husbands to bring along their chorines. And what about that new upstairs maid Junior has his eye on? Dress her up in duds left behind by what's-her-name (yon absent daughter), and she'll make a more than adequate replacement.

Miss Ready—like many others, we'd learn—held the opinion that the whole thing was a high-society stunt, a game of some sort. Like the "charity" scavenger hunts bluebloods stage for their own amusement. Whether they really believed this or were merely using their apparent incredulity to mask meaner feelings of runaway Schadenfreude, it was impossible to tell. For anyone who'd actually spent time among the spoiled youth of the moneyed class, the idea was, at best, far-fetched. Initiative and imagination, which the scheme would have called for in abundance, were not their strong suits.

That evening, after sending his prospective son-in-law to do his weeping at his own home—a Long Island estate he mockingly referred to as Camelot—Rutledge escorted me into his dining room.

"I made some calls this afternoon," he said. "I've been assured that the Navy has a flotilla of destroyers out looking for that airship."

"It would be like trying to find a needle in a haystack. Worse, actually, since their prey will always spot them first. And I doubt they're looking for a confrontation."

"They've also been sending out every seaplane they can get their hands on. As are the French, and the British."

"Certainly a better chance, but few of them can go

any real distance. When we encountered the pirates, they were in the middle of the Atlantic. And by now, they could be off the coast of Brazil."

"What, then?"

"Another airship is the only thing that will catch up to them. Why, if I had a modern ship, and the right crew..." It was the pre-dinner cocktails talking now.

"But where could we get such an airship?" he asked.

"The only one in the country is the *Shenandoah*, commissioned just last fall. I read she was badly damaged in a storm in January. But even if she's out of dry dock, the Navy would never give her up. And if they were forced to go along, it would have to be their show—which means lots of planning and little action."

"I've read the Zeppelin factory is starting to churn them out again."

"They're finishing one for our Navy now. A replacement for those due us as reparations. If we could get hold of that, I doubt there's another airship afloat that would be her match. But we'd need to get it before the Navy takes possession."

"And you could fly it?"

"Oh, yes. With the right crew, of course." Rutledge had come to think me some sort of airship genius, based solely on a lot of near-facts and figures I'd spewed forth over the prior two days. And by the third glass of wine, I was beginning to believe it myself. "However, we'd need to act quickly. You can be sure the Navy already has a captain picked out. And then they'd insist on several months of trials in the air before attempting anything as daring as what we have in mind."

"We don't have several months! Listen, it's imperative Lizzie's wedding go off as planned, on the eighteenth of June.... What I mean to say is, she has her heart set on it. And all the arrangements are made."

"I see." I didn't really. His only child was in the clutches of God knows what sort of menace and he was worried about the deposit he'd put down on the wedding supper.

"Listen, suppose I buy it myself? Offer them a nice profit, and then we organize an expedition along our own lines."

"It would be quite an expensive endeavor...."

"She's my daughter! Besides, that drip she's engaged to is good for millions. Tomorrow we go down to Washington. I'm going to insist on a meeting with the president."

"That could be a tall order."

"I remember on board the *Paris*—when we were having that little... disagreement—you mentioned you knew him."

"Only barely. And I'm afraid it's been a good many years. Before he'd gone to Boston as governor. I'm not entirely sure he'd remember me."

"Well, I can call on Mellon. I helped the Treasury unload a pile of Liberty Bonds during the war. That ought to count for something. You agree, I assume, we're better off going to the top."

"Oh, yes. I don't think there's any doubt about that. We'd never get anywhere with the Navy."

"Let me just make clear once again how important it is that Lizzie is back in time for her wedding. I plan to offer a reward of twenty-five thousand dollars to the man who brings about her safe return. However... I may rescind that offer any time after the eighteenth of June. That last condition is just between you and me, understand."

I understood, all right. *He* was the one doing the fortune hunting.

We were just leaving the table for the billiard room when the butler entered.

"There is a call, sir. From a lady journalist."

"I told you I don't want to speak with any newspapermen—females included."

"Very good, sir. And so I told her. But she informed me she's doing a story for tomorrow's edition in which you feature prominently. She therefore wanted to offer you the opportunity to speak with her."

"She's just fishing. Tell her—"

"Wait," I said. "If I might suggest, it could behoove us to make use of the press for our own purposes. No doubt she *is* just fishing for a story. Well, why not provide her with one? One which serves *our* purposes."

"All right, you talk with her. But don't let her come here.... And be careful what you divulge."

"Don't worry. I've kept my share of secrets." I gave him a wink.

He in turn looked nervously at the butler. He'd talked too much and regretted it. But now it was too late. I thought it an ideal time to ask for a small loan. Not surprisingly, he assented.

The lady journalist on the phone turned out to be Aggie Ready, the sardonic skeptic. She voiced disappointment when told Rutledge was indisposed, but perked up on hearing that my wife was among the booty.

"Would you mind meeting me downtown?" she asked.

"Not at all. Where?"

"Chumley's, on Bedford Street. Know it?"

I did know it. In fact, I'd been forcibly ejected from

the place only a year before. I suppose I could have suggested another rendezvous. But by then I'd been ejected from all the better class of speakeasies, so it hardly seemed to matter.

II

Either Chumley's had a new man at the door or he'd forgotten tossing me out. I ran the lady's name by the barman. He nodded vaguely toward a figure sitting in a secluded corner. Or as secluded as you could find in a place like Chumley's.

She was a funny-looking sheba, wearing a shabby tweed jacket and a skirt of bright checks. A doll-sized hat sat perched atop her mussed mop cradling a moth-eaten canary—its feet aimed forever heavenward. Like all would-be bohemians, she dressed for ironic effect. Unfortunately, her natural features ran along similar lines. Her face was perfectly round and far too small, and the beady black eyes and button nose were drawn to scale. But not so her mouth. That was unequivocally outsized. And as if to accentuate the fact, she'd smeared scarlet gloss haphazardly across her lips.

She sat alone at a little table, but with a gaggle of men hovering about. I assumed they were fellow scribes rather than admirers.

"Match me," she told one.

He obliged, then stepped back into the pack.

She blew smoke rings at the ceiling and watched them disappear into the prevailing haze, pretending not to have noticed my approach. Even after I introduced myself, she turned only slowly. It was a performance, all right.

"So ya came, did ya?" She spoke through only one

side of her mouth, but given the expanse, that was enough.

After instructing me to order a round of drinks, she took out a little notebook. "OK, let's hear what you got."

I gave her a firsthand account of that eventful evening—leaving off the unseemly episode involving the plank. In this version, I heroically clambered down to the promenade deck and into the music room to protect my dear wife. It was only on being clubbed unconscious with the butt end of a cutlass that I'd been stopped. There was a large lump on my temple from where my head had banged on a railing and this lent my yarn verisimilitude.

"You poor dear..."

I took from her tone that she was less than persuaded. She now turned and spoke to the crowd, "All right, boys. Pay up."

One by one, her gaggle of attendants approached the table and deposited five dollars each.

"They didn't believe I could get one of you here. Thought you'd be too broken up. I knew better. You put on a spiffy side, but your story still smells like an overripe garbage scow. How about now you have a shy at givin' up the goods straight? What's your connection with Rutledge?"

"Connection? Just our common plight. We only met on the boat."

She blew a cloud of smoke in my face. "Yeah. And now you're staying at his house. Chummy." She rose from the table. She wasn't five feet tall, and I believe she wore heels. "I'll leave you with these sharks. I already know all I need to." She picked up her winnings and pushed her way out. A moment later, the waiter arrived with a large tray. Apparently, I'd ordered a round for the fourth estate's entire delegation.

"Cynical girl," I said to no one in particular.

"Yeah, but she ain't alone. Something don't jive."

"Such as?"

"Well, such as, why didn't the crew try to shoot the thing down? Must have been full of hydrogen, right?"

"Probably." I thought it wise to leave off mention of steam power, as my tale would be fantastic enough. "But normal rifle bullets go right through with no effect. We learned that during the war."

"Then what about a flare gun? The gas would have gone up in a second."

"Yes, and the S.S. *Paris* a second later. It hovered right above the ship."

"All right, set that aside. How come these pirates take only the swellest girls on the boat, but then make no demands?"

"It's a mystery, what can I say?"

"How about something worth printing? We heard you were investigating on board. You must have learned something. Throw us a bone...."

"Well, one thing that came out: they were almost certainly Orientals."

"You're kidding...."

"No, not at all."

"I thought they all wore masks."

"Yes, clever of them, wasn't it?"

"You're saying they wore masks to cover up the fact they were Oriental?"

"Why else? But there were other clues as well. For one thing, they were all somewhat short. And very polite."

"And that proves they were Chinks?"

"Japanese was our first choice. Not one of them spat the entire time they were aboard."

"He's right. Chinamen spit—at least in my neighborhood, they do."

"What would these Japs be doing in an airship in the Atlantic?"

"What else?" I asked back. "Rum-running! Why, fortunes are being made every hour. Surely I don't need to tell you inkslingers about that?"

"Wouldn't it make more sense to smuggle it to the West Coast?"

"Bringing what? Sake? The money's in champagne and Scotch."

I doubt any of them really bought my scenario, but neither did they care whether it was true or not. What they did care about was the potential for sensation. And I'd dealt them that in spades: a mystery airship, wily Orientals, illicit booze, dagger-wielding pirates, and female virtue in peril. A royal flush for the yellow journalist.

The next afternoon, Rutledge, Congdon, and I arrived in Washington. While the old man met with Andrew Mellon at the Treasury, I brought Congdon with me to the office of one of my old cronies. His name was Baker, another two-striper now, and one of the few of my Academy classmates still on speaking terms with me.

Baker was every bit as lazy and shiftless as I was. And, believe it or not, even more incompetent on the bridge of a ship. But he was also better at avoiding consequences. He worked in naval intelligence and I suppose the secretive nature of the work kept him from being too closely observed.

I gave him a précis of our plan and he answered with a look of pure incredulity.

"If there's a joke in there, I'm not getting it."

"We couldn't be more serious."

"You think they'll just sell you their Zeppelin? Do you have any idea what sort of figures you'd be talking?"

"I'm prepared to write a check for nearly any amount," Congdon announced.

It was my fault for not cautioning him before we arrived. Baker, not surprisingly, assumed I'd brought the millionaire there as part of an elaborate con game. He immediately called in a stenographer to draw up a bill of sale for "one Zeppelin, large."

"Nix that," I told him. "This is on the up and up. My own wife's been taken! You remember dear Sesbania."

"I remember the black eye she gave me."

"She's just not fond of people taking liberties with her backside."

"Well then, I hope those pirates are proper Christians. By the way, congratulations on the nuptials. I hadn't heard."

"Look, can we stick to the matter at hand?" Congdon interrupted.

"What is it exactly you want from me?"

"The status of the *Shenandoah*," I told him. "And a list of which motorized blimps are currently operative. But most importantly, any details you can get on this new Zeppelin: cost of production, delivery date, etc. And whatever other airships are available."

"And for my trouble?"

"One thousand dollars. On delivery of the information by... say... ten o'clock tonight. You'll find us at the Willard."

"That's just eight hours from now. And it's Saturday afternoon...."

"One thousand, cash. Deal?"

"Deal."

In the cab back to the hotel, Congdon voiced some reluctance about bribing a public official.

"You can't be serious? How do you think your family amassed its fortune in the first place?"

"I try not to think about that. Business doesn't interest me. All too sordid. As soon as we're married, I plan to turn over management of the estate to Lizzie's father."

No wonder Rutledge was so keen on the marriage taking place.

Once they'd been apprised who Congdon was, the hotel staff proved more than happy to cash his check.

"Better make it three thousand," I suggested. "There'll almost certainly be other expenses before this is over."

After the cashier counted out my winnings, I handed Congdon five hundreds for his personal use. The episode left me feeling a wee bit awkward. Not for taking the sap's money. But because his lack of competitive spirit made the thing seem so unsporting. I'd taken candy from babies who put up more of a fight.

At dinner that evening, Rutledge reported on his meeting with the Secretary of the Treasury.

"He's arranged a golf outing for tomorrow afternoon with Coolidge's secretary, a fellow named Slemp. He handles all appointments. Mellon suggested that meanwhile you plead our case with the naval aide to the president."

"I don't know about that...."

"You haven't heard the worst of it. I tried calling this naval aide, but apparently he's out of town. So they gave me the name of his assistant. Guess who he is."

"No idea."

"Oh, you know him, all right. Your pal, Lt. Dirk Gilbert. Hell, he'll never OK us."

"It is bad luck.... But I think I just might have the means to persuade him."

Rutledge passed me a wry smile. He knew what I was about.

As we left the table, I suggested we play some cards, to divert our minds. I contented myself with fleecing Congdon, and was careful to make sure Rutledge came out ahead. Threading a needle like that is never easy, but Congdon did what he could to help. He telegraphed his intentions by facial expression alone. It seemed incredible this ripe suck made it through four years of Yale with his fortune intact. If he'd been at the Academy, we'd have picked him clean before he'd finished his plebe year. But we were a more spirited lot than the gazebos you find populating the Ivy League.

It was past midnight when Baker telephoned. He picked me up outside and drove us to the north of town.

"The *Shenandoah* will be in dry dock for another month at least. But from what I hear, they'll never risk her on a venture like yours. Apparently, she holds most of the world's available helium, and that came mighty dear. ZR-3, the ship they're building in Friedrichshafen, isn't due to be completed until August. And the powered blimps have been decommissioned en masse."

"Every one of them?"

"It seems all the explosions finally dampened enthusiasm for hydrogen craft. And it will be years before there's enough helium about. I did hear of another ship, but I couldn't find out much about it. All very secret. A semi-rigid ship of foreign manufacture."

"Where is this?"

"In a hangar, down in Florida. That's all I could learn."

"Interesting. Not as good as a Zeppelin, but far more useful than a blimp. Do you have names of anyone on the crew? I'm sure to know someone."

"There is no crew, at least on record. Nor has it ever been commissioned. Very mysterious."

"Could be just the thing we need."

I handed over his loot and we stopped at a speak out in the woods somewhere.

"Why didn't you mention Gilbert had been assigned to the White House?"

"You didn't ask. Your old nemesis..."

He referred to the time Gilbert brought charges of gross incompetence against me. I was on night watch aboard that torpedo boat in New York Harbor when I mistook a navigational buoy for the conning tower of a U-boat. Luckily, the torpedo was a dud, or the city of New York would have been short one ferry. Baker insisted I recount the episode once more for his entertainment.

"Chalk it up to the fogs of war," I concluded.

"If I remember right, it was shown there had been no fog at all that night."

"I meant my head. I'd just returned from a twenty-four-hour leave. Is Gilbert still with Kate?"

"Yes. They have a place in Foggy Bottom. I can give you the number."

"Thanks. I think I'll look them up tomorrow."

III

While sharing a late breakfast with my patrons, I told them about the mystery craft hidden down in Florida.

"And you think that will fill the bill?" Rutledge asked.

"Well, it's our best chance, certainly."

"All right. I'll make an offer." Then, turning to Congdon: "Or, rather, you will, my boy."

"Yes, of course."

"And you might also make a contribution to Coolidge's campaign," I suggested. "I hear this is expected to be the most expensive election ever."

"Yes, yes. All right. But this all better be for something."

I called the Gilberts' just after noon. Kate answered.

"I never thought I'd hear from you again...."

The last time we'd seen each other, we were commiserating over her husband. That was years before, not long after their marriage. How she got hooked up with that prig, I never understood. A comely colleen, Kate was: high-chested and round-bottomed, endowed with big brown eyes, a lush blonde mane (by then bobbed to regulation length), and a very agreeable disposition. A stand-up girl, all right—and even better lying down.

She told me Gilbert had gone directly from church to his office, which only confirmed what a colossal ass he was. "He'll be away all afternoon...."

From her tone, I surmised she felt in renewed need of commiseration. I told her that I was married myself now, not wanting to undermine the part I'd been playing. But her disappointed reaction left me feeling decidedly ungallant. And then I remembered my reputed bride's serene response to her abduction. Recognizing perfume, she of all people must have known what those Amazons had in mind....

"I'll see you in ten minutes," I told her.

You might find it surprising a girl I hadn't seen for seven years was so keen on a reunion. But I've always had a way with women. And I can lay it all to my high school Latin teacher—though I never did her.

She was a young widow, and treated me with a chilly aloofness. She rarely displayed warmth toward anyone, but was always particularly cool toward me. One day she announced she needed someone to split a cord of wood. Her offer was absolutely paltry—two bits, if I remember. But I was anxious to get on her good side, for various reasons. One being that I was in danger of failing Latin. Another being that I found her damnably attractive.

It was September, a warm Saturday afternoon, and I out there banging away with my wedges—shirtless, and moist with perspiration—when she appeared with some lemonade. She watched as I downed it, and then asked me what seemed a most curious question.

"Tell me, Pluribus, can you touch your nose with your tongue?"

I could, in fact, and my demonstration pleased her.

Ten minutes later, she was giving me a lesson in female anatomy. She knew just what she wanted and she wasn't shy about asking for it. While I went to work below deck, she began conjugating Latin verbs. Whether this was merely meant to provide cover for a nosy neighbor or a necessary step in bringing her to the revelatory moment, I can't say with any certainty. However, to this day, a woman reciting Latin in a similar breathless tone will cause me to break out in a sweat.

She never allowed my nether regions near hers, nor did we even kiss. But once she was herself satisfied with events, she would reach for mine. She had a graceful hand, and it was usually all over in the blink of an eye. (I wasn't sixteen when it started, and my fuse short.) Then it was, "On your way, Pluribus."

I did manage to pass Latin, thanks partly to her chanting. But she continued treating me with a coolness bordering on disdain. Well, you can't have your cake and eat it too. Or should it be vice versa?

Kate didn't chant Latin. She favored one particular syllable: "*Tchaw!*"

She'd utter it whenever I'd hit the bull's-eye six or seven times in a row. Then she'd remember she was a good Catholic girl and her knees would snap together. I learned to take the "*Tchaw!*" as both encouragement and warning. But it was exhausting work. Not only was it necessary for me to move my head out of the way at the sound of the "*Tchaw!*," I then had to persuade her thighs apart for the next flight. Don't think I'm complaining— when she was good and ready she pulled me up and I got mine, all right.

It wasn't until after four that we left the bedroom— though it must be admitted for half an hour of that we were napping. She told me she was now determined to leave Gilbert, but worried she'd only end up with some- one else unable to see the virtues of female fulfillment. I explained to her, as I had to so many other women, it was just a matter of being insistent from the very beginning. Any man worth his salt would want to please her; he was just likely to need detailed instructions.

Then I counted out ten hundreds. "This is for your escape."

"A thousand dollars? I couldn't ask you..."

"Consider it a gift. Or maybe a gift for the next man who hears the '*Tchaw!*'."

"Tchaw? I don't know what you mean."

"Well... never mind."

With her permission, I telephoned her husband, pretending to be calling from the hotel. He begrudgingly allowed me to come by his office.

Our meeting began as badly as you might expect. I told him our plan, while he interrupted with periodic expostulations of scorn and abuse.

"You think the Navy would turn an airship over to *you,* of all people?" he jeered.

It was then I alluded to that photographic evidence I mentioned earlier.

"He certainly was an amenable old billy, wasn't he?" I said.

That wiped the grin off his face. But it only served to make him more disagreeable.

In truth, all I could achieve was his embarrassment. Navy regulations didn't cover farm animals. So I hazarded a try at something more serious.

"I was wondering, old sport, how you could manage a first-class berth on a premier liner drawing the pay of a lieutenant."

"What has that to do with you?"

The change in his complexion told me I'd hit pay dirt. "As a taxpayer, it has a great deal to do with me. Someone was repaying a kindness you'd done him, wasn't that it? A generous shipbuilder?"

"I don't know what you're talking about. The idea's absurd. I bought that ticket myself. Anyway, do you have any idea what you're asking? If I were to back you up on this, my career would be on the line. And besides, there aren't any airships currently in operation."

"What about the one down in Florida?"

"How do you know about that?" Now he sounded

downright anxious. Which meant, I assumed, I'd hit upon a secret worth knowing.

"I have my sources."

"That... That's a special case. You should never have been told about it. But I doubt it would suit your needs, regardless. If I were you, I'd forget I ever heard of it."

"Too late for that, I'm afraid. Just help us get in to see Coolidge—you don't need to endorse the idea."

"I couldn't get you an appointment if I wanted to. Hell, I've only met the man twice myself."

"Do what you can. Or I'll give my story to a reporter of my acquaintance. She writes for the *New York World* and is even less credulous than I am."

His reply wasn't a friendly one. I felt confident I'd given him little room to maneuver; he could either accede to my request, or face the risk of court-martial. But he had one more card to play.

At dinner, Rutledge reported on his golf outing. Slemp, the president's secretary, had listened intently to his proposal, but insisted he knew nothing about an airship in Florida. He promised to check into the matter. Then, at mention of a sizable contribution to the upcoming campaign, he invited both Rutledge and Congdon to lunch at the White House the next day.

About ten that evening, I received a call at the hotel. It came from an old acquaintance named Timken who had likewise served aboard the blimps. He'd been senior to me and was now a lieutenant commander with a berth at the Navy Department. He suggested we go out for a drink. I knew it wasn't a social invitation—he'd never treated me with anything but contempt. And since Gilbert had almost certainly initiated the meeting, I fully expected to be bullied. Just not what came later....

CHAPTER 3.

WILBUR THE WILLING

Timken drove us out toward the Navy Yard. He told me whatever I'd learned about the airship in Florida had best be forgotten. I didn't tell him about Rutledge's conversation with the president's secretary, only what I'd told Gilbert, that it might be too late.

"Well, you had better just see that it isn't!"

"Or what?" I asked, dismissively.

His tone implied a physical dimension to the threat. But being the larger, I'd have the advantage in a fair fight. Not that I'd ever in my life fought fairly.

He calmed himself, and the conversation became less heated. When we were just outside the gates of the yard, he turned and continued east. It was a neighborhood of industrial buildings and warehouses. I actually felt relieved. Until then, I'd feared he was taking us to the officers' club, a thoroughly dry establishment. Now I assumed we were headed to another well-camouflaged speakeasy. But I'd assumed wrong.

He stopped along a dark side street. There were three others waiting, younger officers I'd never met before. When one pulled me from the car, I offered no resistance. But once outside, I kneed him in the groin and shot down an alley. Two of them charged after me. I couldn't outrun them for long, so as soon as I felt sure I was out of sight, I hopped over a fence.

A gigantic hound came lunging at me. Judging from his disposition, an ill-fed gigantic hound. Just in the nick of time, I managed to hurdle a second fence catty-corner to the first. This brought me out on another desolate street. There were headlights coming toward me from both directions. I ran to the building opposite and found the door locked. I'd just put an elbow through a window when Timken laid his hand on my shoulder. I gave him a solid punch to the jaw, and when he spun to starboard, a dirty one to his port-side kidney. He was down, but not the goon who'd been driving a truck from the opposite direction. He knocked me hard against the wall. Then his two comrades showed up.

While they took turns reconfiguring my anatomy, their senior officer collected himself. He took a couple cheap shots while the others held my arms. But he preferred to stand by and watch approvingly. Grinning, in fact. When they all felt the job had been done properly, they flung me into the back of the truck. The last thing I remembered was being tossed onto the street several blocks short of the Willard.

A bellboy helped me upstairs and summoned the hotel doctor. No broken limbs, luckily, but a few ribs had slipped their moorings. When Rutledge and Congdon came by in the morning, I told them some bilge about running into trouble outside a speakeasy. I didn't want them to get cold feet and miss their lunch date at the White House.

It was almost three when they returned. Along with them was a waiter carting a bucket of champagne. Coolidge had been all for the scheme, just five hundred thousand for the airship, and another fifty for ye olde slush fund. In addition, I would be reinstated as a reserve officer and have command—but without pay, or a budget. However, as long as Congdon's pen held out, I didn't foresee a problem on that front.

He gave no evidence of feeling the pinch, just impatience. "How soon can we get out to sea?"

"Well, we'll need a crew...."

"They're providing a crew," Rutledge said. "Enlisted men only, no officers."

"All the better," I told him. "Gives me a chance to run things right." Once again, mere bravado. I didn't even know what sort of airship we'd gotten hold of, let alone whether I could fly the thing.

Next, Congdon informed us he'd be coming along.

"I'd hoped you would," I told him. Where he went, his checkbook was sure to follow.

We spent the next twenty-four hours assembling our duffels. Congdon bought himself a couple smart-looking yachting outfits, while I returned to the uniform of a lieutenant, junior grade.

"What about swords?" he asked.

He stood about five foot six, when shod, and I suppose he hoped a sword would lend him a military bearing. In that regard it fell short. But he was footing the bill, and we were, after all, pursuing pirates. So swords it was.

We were at the station, waiting to board the overnight train to Jacksonville, when Baker came by.

"Heard you had a rough time the other night."

"No worse than what those bluenosers meted out back in Crabtown." There were some among my classmates unable to appreciate inventiveness at the card table. Though, in truth, I'd never been beaten quite so thoroughly.

"Well, if it's any consolation, Gilbert et al. have landed in the soup."

"What do you mean?"

"That airship down in Florida. They weren't keeping

it a secret for military reasons. It turns out Coolidge and his people knew nothing about it. He's against spending more money on the things."

"Then where'd this ship in Florida come from?"

"A sister ship of the *Roma*."

"The *Roma?* She was an Army ship."

"Yes, but after the *Roma* had been delivered, the Navy insisted on ordering one of the same design for themselves. Theirs arrived just after the accident."

"What accident?" Congdon asked.

"Back in '22," Baker told him. "The *Roma* crashed and burned. Not even a year after she was acquired from the Italians. Thirty-four dead, wasn't it?" he asked me.

"Eleven survivors," I said with all the sanguinity I could muster.

"Could be a bit risky," Baker added rather needlessly.

"It's just a chance we'll have to take," Congdon assured him. Up until this point, probably the riskiest endeavor he'd ever undertaken was to consume oysters in an r-less month.

"Anyway, Coolidge was happy to be rid of the thing, and at a profit," Baker went on. "Gilbert and friends will likely be posted to mosquito-boat duty in some pestilent backwater. At least until the plucking board sends them their papers. Well, good luck to you."

I shook his hand, but his too-satisfied expression gave him away.

"You knew all this from the beginning, didn't you?"

"The broad outlines."

"Never trust a sea lawyer."

"You're one to talk. Remember that Reo you sold me just after graduation?"

"I'd forgotten all about it."

"Well, I hadn't. Didn't make it past the gates."

"Holding grudges is beneath an officer in the United States Navy."

"That's why it's important to get even at the first opportunity. I've waited nine years. Bon voyage."

His news had certainly given me something to think about on the trip down. Take a faultily designed airship, keep it out of sight for two years—with likely no maintenance performed whatsoever—and fill it full of highly combustible gas. My feelings toward the adventure were becoming mixed. Then I thought again of Congdon's checkbook. And Rutledge's twenty-five-thousand-dollar reward. And Sesbania's undergarments—not to mention the old girl herself, of course.

At supper, Congdon asked for further details of the *Roma*'s incineration. I told him it'd been a freak accident, but that fell a little short of the truth. She was bought at a time of airship euphoria—everyone wanted one. The Navy had purchased a model based on the Zeppelin from the Brits, and the Army birdmen felt left out. Meanwhile, the Italians—who had built the *Roma* only to have the war end before it was completed—were looking for a buyer.

The Army sent over a group to determine if it should be bought. One of those men—one who was lucky enough to survive the crash—later admitted to me that during the one test flight that time allowed for, they'd all consumed an outrageous amount of wine.

I planned to follow a similar course.

II

The base at Pensacola was a naval air station, so it wasn't illogical that the airship would be stored there.

The post commander had been alerted to our arrival and sent an officer named Erickson to meet our train. Erickson was another lieutenant commander, and about ten years my senior. We knew each other only vaguely; seaplanes were his bailiwick. He whisked us straightaway to a giant hangar on the edge of the station with nary a word along the way.

"Well, this is where I leave you," he said politely, then did just that.

The hangar was huge, but in poor repair. The first door I tried was rusted shut. Not an auspicious sign. We had better luck around back. A small office lay exposed behind a screen door. And at a desk in that office sat a chief petty officer. I knocked lightly as we entered. He'd fallen asleep with his feet up on the desk and an issue of *Capt. Billy's Whiz Bang* in his lap. I was well familiar with the publication, a monthly compendium of prurient humor popular among high school sophomores and servicemen of all ranks.

Rather than shout at the man, I cleared my throat. I've always been sympathetic with layabouts, whatever their grade. Not so Rutledge, apparently. He walked over and spun the chair around.

"Hey! You son-of-a—" On seeing my uniform, the CPO cut short what promised to be a string of epithets and snapped to attention.

"At ease, Chief. I suppose you know why we're here."

"Oh... yes, sir. It's about..." He made a cursory search of the top of the desk, hoping maybe for some clue among the mess of paperwork. "Ah... no... no, sir, I can't say I do."

"Odd. What's your name?"

"Cartwright, sir."

"Well, Cartwright, I'm Lieutenant Van Slyke and I've come to take possession of the airship."

"Wilbur, sir?"

"Wilbur? I wasn't aware it had ever been christened."

"Well, not officially christened. But the boys got sick of referring to him as SC-aught-three."

"I thought ships were always shes," Congdon noted.

"Well, usually. Wilbur's a special case."

"Named for a comrade lost in the war?"

"Lost in battle, you could say."

"Leaving the cognomen aside, what's the current status of the ship?" I asked.

"Status?"

"Is it air-worthy?"

"Under what circumstances, sir?"

"What do you mean, under what circumstances? Is the envelope in good repair?"

"Oh, yes, sir."

"So you've tested it with hydrogen recently?"

"Hydrogen, sir? That's dangerous stuff."

"Then how do you know the envelope is sound?"

"Well, I guess it comes down to what you mean by sound, sir. We pump it full of air every few months.... Just did it back in November. No, I'm a liar. September it was. Part of the regular ninety-day routine."

"Nine-month, you mean."

"How's that?"

"Never mind. Why don't we just see it for ourselves?"

"Right now, sir?"

"Yes, now. It's here in the hangar, isn't it?"

"Oh, yes. It's just been a while since we showed him.... This way."

He led us through a door and into the large cavern of the hangar. Dim light came in through a row of small, filthy windows near the top of one side.

"Lights?" I prompted.

"Are you sure, sir?"

"How else will we see it?"

"Yeah." He walked down to an electrical box and flung a large lever upward. A couple dozen large lights came on. Then we heard a series of pops. Once the explosions ended, just a handful of the bulbs remained shining. Not nearly enough to illuminate the giant space, but more than adequate to see Wilbur was in a very sorry state.

"A bit... flaccid, isn't it?" Congdon asked.

"That's just the word, sir. See, Wilbur was a member of the crew a year or so back, machinist's mate, third class. He had a reputation... among the working ladies in town.... Always came in D&D...."

"D&D?"

"Very drunk and very disorderly, sir. Well, when it came time to complete the transaction..."

"Yes, we get the picture, Chief. Let's just hope Wilbur can hold his hydrogen better than his liquor. How about the engines?"

"Should be six of them, sir."

"What do you mean, should be?"

"Well, they arrived disassembled back in '22, packed in grease. The crates are over on the far side there, with the parts of the rudder."

"Parts of the rudder? So the controls can't be tested?"

"Oh, they seem all right.... From what we can tell."

As he led the way under the shadow of the ship, I stayed behind and took a quick nip from my flask. His words came as portents of my early demise.

When I caught up, the others were entering the ship. As with the *Roma,* there was no gondola per se, but rather a corridor running the length of the keel. Cartwright guided us through the crew's quarters, and then the galley, and finally into the control room. There we found three enlisted men playing cards by candlelight. They spat out the cigars they'd been chomping and snapped to attention.

"The lieutenant wants to check the controls. Show him, Dombrowski."

One of the men fell out and led me to a panel of cords and knobs.

"I think these here are used to vent gas, sir. Assuming there *was* gas. An' these here to drop ballast..."

"Assuming there was ballast?"

"Yes, sir. These others I haven't been able to figure out. Over here is the telegraph to the enginemen, assuming there were enginemen..."

"...or engines."

"Yes, sir. The helm here works just like any ship..."

"...assuming the rudder's been attached."

"Well, sure, sir. A ship's gotta have a rudder."

"Yes, so I'm told.... Cartwright, have your men assemble outside in front of the hangar. How many are there altogether?"

"Including me, sir? Three. Perkins here is just visiting."

"From where?"

"I'm a cook's mate, sir."

"Well, we'll need one. Consider yourself reassigned. I'll call your CO. Now, everyone outside."

I took Congdon and Rutledge into the office for a

confab and another belt from the flask. The old man had been curiously quiet since our arrival and I thought some encouragement might be in order, however unfounded.

"It's not as bad as it looks," I told them. "I've seen craft in far worse shape than this."

"That flew?" Rutledge asked.

"Oh, yes." Well, had flown. "I suggest you go check us into the hotel. Then, send a wire to Washington and remind them about the crewmen they promised. I'm not sure these gobs are adequate to the task. We need people with real flight experience."

"And me?" Congdon asked.

"Well, as procurement officer, you have some work to do here. We'll need hydrogen, a lot of it, and fuel, and probably a slew of parts. Cartwright can point you in the right direction."

Outside, I inspected my pathetic command. Clearly this was a dumping ground for lifers without talents or prospects. Of course, when the chips are down, and the ship's in mortal peril, it's often the unassuming seaman who saves the day. Or so I've read. So far, I'd pretty ably managed to avoid ships in mortal peril.

"Let's open the hangar doors and see the thing in daylight."

"Open the hangar doors, sir?"

"Yes, is there a problem with that?"

"Wouldn't know, sir. My orders were to never open the hangar doors under any circumstances."

The men spent the remainder of that day and most of the next prying the huge doors open with the help of a steam winch. Rutledge's mood hadn't improved, but at least Congdon had taken to his task. He had a talent for writing checks.

While he worked his pen, I gathered together all the documentation on the ship I could find. There was quite a lot: manuals, inventories, diagrams, etc. Unfortunately, nearly all in Italian. I noted this to Cartwright.

"Yes, did pose a problem. But Dombrowski can make some of it out."

"Dombrowski's Italian?"

"Oh, yeah. Mother's all wop. He can read it as good as he can American."

I learned the worth of that recommendation at lunch, when I witnessed the Italian asking Cartwright's help with a rhetorical point raised in *Capt. Billy's Whiz Bang*.

I ate the midday meal with the men, partly as a show of comradeship, but mainly because I hadn't been invited to eat with the base officers. A highly unusual situation for a visiting officer. I attributed it to petty jealousy at my having been given command of Wilbur. One positive emerging from my banishment was that Mrs. Erickson, the lieutenant commander's wife, brought me a picnic basket of provisions. She told me the others were just being small-minded, and I agreed with her wholeheartedly, as good manners demanded.

I was surprised she even remembered me. We'd met just once, in New Jersey. The commanding officer of the base had held a golfing party. Erickson, under the misapprehension wives were invited, brought his along. Then, on realizing his faux pas, he relegated her to the parking lot.

Fortunately for us both, thirteen officers had shown up, making three foursomes and a spare. I gallantly ceded my spot on the roster, and took one beside her in the car. She was older than me, probably mid-thirties then. But she had the classic sort of good looks some women take to the grave: tall and trim, with high cheekbones, crystal-blue eyes, and hair more white than blonde.

Nothing happened that day—I don't think I even made a pass at her. We just drove out to the shore and walked along the sand, talking little. I think she had it in her mind I'd made a sacrifice of some sort, perhaps even been ordered to escort her. But I'd already been tiring of the company of men—and always despised golf. Four hours of addressing, kissing, and finessing, and just to get into a succession of purely allusive holes.

Following lunch, Wilbur was towed out onto the field. The bright Florida sun did nothing for his looks. With the help of a derrick, we remounted the rudder, and then set about reassembling the engines. Two days later, the rail cars of hydrogen arrived. The crew seemed reluctant to handle the stuff, so I procured a case of Cuban beer from a blind pig in town and served it at lunch. Happily, the envelope did hold the gas—at least as well as the men did their beer.

The following day, the complement of crew arrived. There were eighteen of them, all formerly assigned to the motorized blimps. Two I was on familiar terms with and knew to be thoroughly unreliable. I held out hopes for the others—but only until learning every last man of them had been released from the brig on condition of volunteering. Fifteen were in for relatively benign offenses: drunk and disorderly, AWOL, petty thievery, etc. The sixteenth, a big ugly thug, had been charged with striking an officer. Not terribly auspicious, but then there's no denying that big ugly thugs come in very handy when confronting pirates.

III

Ironically, it was the two men not from the brig, Blight and Woese, who worried me most. Not only did they know about my near-torpedoing of the municipal ferry—and my more successful one of the admiral's wife—they'd witnessed the stampede of circus elephants firsthand. I took them into the office.

"I'm surprised to see you men."

"Not half as surprised as we are to see you, sir," Blight told me. "We thought you'd been... well, retired."

"Yes, but I was needed for this rather special assignment. I understood you were all to be volunteers."

"By Navy thinking. Open your mouth to breathe, or blink an eye—you volunteered."

"I see. Well, look, it might not do much for the men's morale if they were to learn the details of... certain incidents. After all, that's water under the bridge."

"What about *our* morale, sir?"

"I think I can arrange a little something extra in the pay envelope."

"What about rations?"

"What about them?"

"Rum, I mean."

"Oh, we're doing what we can. And once we're out past the twelve-mile limit..."

"Will we be? What exactly is our mission?"

"Our mission? I'll be addressing the entire crew about that in the morning."

The conversation had given me an inspiration. One of an officer's chief concerns is keeping the ranks motivated. Patriotism sometimes works. Comradeship is better. And self-preservation better still. But rescuing society dames and enriching the ship's captain weren't likely to rate very high. I needed something that would appeal to their baser instincts.

After roll the next morning, I assembled the men in a corner of the hangar.

"Now, what I'm about to tell you is top secret. The success of our mission depends on it."

They were looking rather skeptical. Particularly Albertson, the bird who'd had some experience ironing out difficulties with his officers.

"We've been charged with going out and interrupting the rum-runners' bases of operation."

"Where's that?"

"Their ships' holding station outside the limits, island sanctuaries, things like that."

"Why would we want to do that?"

"Well, to enforce the constitution of the United States, of course.... *And* to confiscate, and eventually destroy—one way or another—their stocks of liquor."

It took some further hinting to bring them around. Reading between the lines isn't a talent universal among Navy ranks. But once they caught on, they took to the idea with enthusiasm.

Not so Congdon, however. He pulled me into the office. "I haven't been spending all this money just to provide that band of rejects with free rum!"

"Quiet down, or our band of rejects is liable to hear you. All we need to do is take on an occasional rum-runner, which we're bound to meet up with along the way. Remember, we'll need them in the game when we come across those pirates."

"I suppose you're right. But will they be any good to us if they're always half-drunk?"

"Don't worry. I know what I'm doing." More brava-do, of course. But I'd seen the crew work sober and it seemed unlikely their being half-drunk could bring about much of a drop in efficiency.

By then, Rutledge had traveled back to New York. And Congdon was spending his free time writing trite couplets to his lost sweetheart. Worse, if he found me within earshot, he insisted on sharing them. So I enter-tained myself with nightly tours of Pensacola's speakeas-ies. Just shacks, most of them. But their patrons more than made up for the lack of amenities with a near insa-tiable capacity for both illicit liquor and scandalous amusements.

I returned to the hotel early the next morning in a condition just this side of unconsciousness. There, wait-ing for me in my room, I found Aggie Ready. She'd fallen asleep on the bed, so I went about pulling off her shoes, to make her more comfortable. She woke spitting fire.

"Hey! What the hell d'ya think you're doing?"

"Sorry." I fell into a chair and started taking my own shoes off.

"Now what are you doing?"

"Preparing for bed."

"Forget it, *sport*. I wouldn't give you the time of day."

"That's too bad. But I'm still going to bed."

"Not yet, you ain't. I want some answers."

"Answers to what?"

"I've got most of it worked out, but some parts ain't clear."

"I'm not sure I follow you."

"Rutledge is in a fix. He made a big play on some foreign bonds, and on margin. If he doesn't come up with some serious money by the first of July, he'll be takin' a dive in the crimson pool. But I guess you knew that."

"No, but I suspected something like it."

"I also know about his daughter and Congdon. And I know *he's* richer than Croesus. I tried talking to him last night and got nowhere."

"What is it you want to know?"

"Somehow Rutledge staged this thing, the whole kidnapping nonsense, and he's using it to get Congdon's money."

"You're off the track there. The kidnapping was real. Rutledge wants nothing more than to get his daughter back and marry her off to Congdon's fortune."

"Then what're all the shenanigans with this airship? I got it from an informant that knows, the whole thing's a joke. Everyone expects it to crash and burn, and some are even hoping for it."

"Like who?"

"Cal and company. They figure one more disaster and there won't be any more talk about airships. And then there's the brass hats. The entire Department of the Navy seems to have it in for you, personally. *And* I know why: I got a guy to give me a peek at your record."

"Outside of a few minor blemishes..."

"Aw, give it a rest! I figure you and Rutledge are working a con on the fiancé. What is it, kickbacks on all these checks he's writing? From what I hear, he's been pretty free with the green. And all this nonsense about your wife being captive, and missing her so. Meanwhile, I find you with your hands all over me!"

"Just your shoes."

"Yeah... for a start." She lit a cigarette. "I did a little checking, friend, and no one remembers you even having a wife. Your berth outbound to Southampton last year was a single."

"She was my fiancée then. We just hadn't made it public. We married in London, last November." I displayed the ring I wore.

She seemed unimpressed. "Yeah? Well, I bet you ain't been faithful for a week.... Oh, I saw you squirm there. Ain't you something? How much did it put you out?"

"That's a slanderous thing to say!" Could she have found out about the thousand I'd given Kate?

"Is it?"

"Yes, you've just maligned one of the finest wives in this man's Navy."

"But not *your* wife."

"You're splitting hairs. The point is, a fine woman has been wronged."

"Yeah? How fine? Wha'd she set you back?"

"Damn fine. And that's all I'll say on the matter. Now I'm going to bed. You're welcome to do as you please."

"Keep dreaming, bimbo."

She went and stood in front of the mirror, trying to straighten herself up. But that was too tall an order. Grooming wasn't her strong suit, and her nap on the bed did nothing to improve the presentation.

"So long," she said at the door. "And just you wait. I'll get to the bottom of this—with you or without you."

A strange girl, all right.

The next afternoon, we took Wilbur up for his inaugural flight. As a matter of safety, I kept us to just a few hundred feet. This had the added benefit of terrorizing women, small children, and livestock, thereby bringing much cheer to the crew. We hugged the coast for this first run, but on each successive day we flew higher and further out to sea.

No one was as surprised as I was at how well things were progressing. At least for the moment....

CHAPTER 4.

FIRST FORAYS

The evening after our fourth flight, I went out celebrating with a vivacious young lady of my recent acquaintance. She called herself Obligin' Nell—and I'd every reason to believe her. During a pause between bouts, she happened to mention that a liquor wholesaler among her intimate circle (an understandably large one) maintained a storehouse on the Dry Tortugas, just a few hours' flight from Pensacola.

The next day, I sent Congdon off to Jacksonville on a contrived errand. I suspected he'd object to what I had in mind. In the meantime, the ship was readied, and early that evening, we cast off. Only when we were well out to sea did I reveal the details of our mission to the crew. I need hardly tell you, they responded with the keenness of spirit one would expect from dedicated seamen of the United States Navy.

I timed our approach so we'd arrive near dawn. At about half past four, we sighted the beacon of the Tortuga lighthouse, and an hour later, a group of buildings on one of the keys. A dozen of the crew repelled down to man the lines. Then, by venting a goodly quantity of hydrogen, I brought the ship slowly down.

So surprised were they by our appearance, the key's inhabitants put up no resistance whatsoever. Our first engagement and we won the day without firing a shot. Granted, the fact that it was a scientific research station we'd stormed, and not a rum-runner's stronghold, may have stacked the deck in our favor. Nonetheless, a victory is a victory.

And fortunately, the men of science were more amused than angry.

"You want Bird Key," one told me. "But I believe I heard them fleeing at your approach. They keep a speed-boat docked there."

"Well, that's damned disappointing. My men have been itching for a fight. Still, we'll need to see that their stocks are destroyed."

In exchange for a share of the haul, they allowed us the use of a boat to ferry the liquor from one key to the other. They were scientists, not Puritans.

The cache lay hidden among the plethora of graves dotting the island. The Dry Tortugas had hosted a rather brutal prison during the Civil War, and from all appearances, Bird Key was its burying ground. We uncovered several dozen cases of liquor, and no fewer than five skulls. The place certainly had an undeniable pirate-like atmosphere. But luckily, no live ones materialized.

A good time was had by all that evening—men of science and gobs alike. And a mere three days later, the crew had sobered up enough to take to the air again. I'd hoped to bring some of the stock back to base, but that wasn't meant to be.

Congdon was angry at having been left behind. But not nearly so livid as the gentleman whose booty we had consumed. His name was Diamondback McGhee, which I learned when he and three of his associates introduced themselves as I made my way back to the hotel late that night. It seems Nell had obliged *him* by providing my name.

Back then, Pensacola was sparing in its use of street lights, and marauders had little trouble finding a dark stretch in which to surprise their victims. They came at me from three sides. While two of them pinned me to a wall, the third went at it. When he tired, they did a little do-si-do and a fresh man had his turn. The feeling of déjà vu was almost as intense as the pain itself.

Mr. McGhee—or Diamondback, as his friends called him—spent the entire time attending to his manicure. He asked that I not think him standoffish—it was only that he had a weak stomach and preferred to avoid the sight of blood. I told him I shared his feelings. He suggested I close my eyes.

As you may well have guessed, I've received quite a number of beatings in my time. And from men in all walks of life. So it pains me to admit, in spite of the pride I've always taken in the uniform, a beating at the hands of the U.S. Navy is nothing compared to that at the hands of Pensacola rum-runners. Rest assured, however: your hero is nothing if not resilient. A few days in the hospital and I could almost walk on my own.

It was on my third day there that Mrs. Erickson came by. She very diplomatically made no reference to how I'd come by my injuries—which saved me the trouble of lying. But she did tell me they hadn't been dressed properly. She then proceeded to do them herself. Well, dressing wounds inevitably involves a good deal of handling, which in somewhat different circumstances might be called caressing, or petting—even, perhaps, fondling. And given the thoroughness of my assailants, there were few areas of my body not requiring attention.

Inhibition has never been among my weak points. But there was something about her—a quiet sort of dignified elegance—which made it impossible for me to take the initiative. So I was greatly relieved when she did. It came very tentative, at first. She kissed my swollen hand, as she would a child's. But I sensed she was on the brink of something unfamiliar and uncharacteristically reckless. Using my free hand, I helped her over the precipice.

I spent an unusual amount of time on the caressing, petting, and fondling. Partly as repayment in kind, and partly because she'd clearly not gotten enough of it at home. It came as no surprise that Erickson was a prisoner of convention, and an inept one at that. But I was nonetheless astonished at how little acquainted she was personally with her little Viking in the longboat. I took it upon myself to introduce them.

As I worked, I remembered that she had told me at our first meeting how much she missed her family and friends back home. Sparking this memory was her recitation of the Moorhead, Minnesota, telephone directory. I'd gotten her through the Andersons, Carlsons, and Hansens (all the way, in fact, to Johansen, Sven G.), when someone threw open the door.

A moment of silence followed, then a man's voice: "Oh, sorry, Doctor, ma'am. Wrong room."

I was under the sheet and apparently he thought I was working in a medical capacity. Mrs. Erickson seemed either not to have noticed the intrusion or not to have cared, but proceeded right on through the Nelsons, Olsons, and Petersons. She let me finish things in the customary fashion, and left little doubt she would have been happy to permit an immediate rematch were I up to it. But we were once more interrupted, this time by my nurse, Alice. She'd come to warn me—a little late—that her father was on the way to have a word with me.

In all fairness to the girl's professional reputation, I should note she'd never been allowed to replace my dressings without distraction. She was a randy little minx, but like Kate, a woman of few sounds. Her sole response to my undertaking was to periodically repeat the syllables "tee-hee," and always in the exact same pitch. As a matter of fact, that was her response to almost every proposal I'd put to her.

Just now, however, she wasn't in a tee-heeing mood. Not so naïve as her father, she had no trouble appraising the situation, and promptly determined I was fit enough to leave her care, which she explained by tossing my things out the second-story window.

Back at the hotel, I found Congdon waiting. He was adamant that we begin our search for the pirates in earnest. Since I was now equally keen to leave the Panhandle, I agreed.

"We'll make for Lakehurst," I told him.

"New Jersey?"

"It's the main airship station and much nearer to where we encountered the pirates at sea. We can resupply there before heading out."

The next morning, as soon as we were airborne, I informed the men we'd be crossing over to the Georgia coast. "From there, we'll head north along the legal limit and board any ships we find at anchor."

The rum-runners were bringing their liquor ashore in secluded coves, isolated beaches, etc., using speedboats capable of evading the larger Coast Guard craft. But the speedboats could only travel so far. The solution was to post ships just beyond the territorial limit, and hence the reach of U.S. law. But I've never had much use for limits, territorial or otherwise.

While I'd been dallying at the hospital, I'd had the men practicing assaults from the air, using the techniques exhibited by the pirates who'd waylaid the S.S. *Paris*. This would save us having to land the ship and expending valuable hydrogen. Wilbur required fifteen men just to keep him aloft, so there'd be only eight of us to make the descent. We spotted our first prey the next morning off Charleston—a leaky old schooner, manned by a half-dozen sleepy men who'd evidently been pilfering from the stores.

There were several Thompson submachine gunners amongst us and they made quite a show of shooting up the deck. In no time, we had the bleary-eyed crew subdued. But now came the difficult part. We had only so much spare capacity on the airship and needed to limit ourselves to two dozen cases. While these were winched up, the eight of us did our damnedest to put a dent in the remainder.

Late that evening, we arrived in Lakehurst to a reception that fell well short of welcoming. When we radioed for landing instructions, we were waved off.

"What's the problem?" Congdon asked.

"Those cream puffs have developed a phobia for hydrogen," I told him.

"What will we do now?"

"There's another naval air station nearby.... We'll make for there."

"How far?"

"Just up across the bay... Rockaway." I tried to say it sotto voce, but apparently didn't try hard enough.

"Rockaway?" The anxious query echoed through the ship.

"What's so ominous about Rockaway?" Congdon asked.

"The D-6 disaster..." Blight told him. "Three airships... gone in the wink of an eye...."

"*Whoosh!*" Woese added theatrically.

"They were just careless. Using antiquated designs," I assured them. "This ship is state-of-the-art. Now, buck up. You don't want Mr. Congdon here to get the idea he's hired on a crew of nancy boys. Remember our mission... and what we're after."

I was alluding to the rum, of course, but Congdon unhelpfully muddied the waters by adding some tripe about women's virtue being at stake. If there was one thing unlikely to motivate a crew like ours, it was upholding women's virtue. They spent their every leave trying to subvert it.

To avoid the risk of another turndown, I opted not to radio Rockaway until our landing was a fait accompli. I'd landed blimps there a number of times and knew the geography well. It was dark by the time we passed Sandy Hook, but the lights of New York promised to make orientation easy. Until, that is, a thick fog rolled in.

Thirty minutes later, Congdon made the excited assertion that I had missed the mark.

"Nonsense," I told him. "I know this approach like the back of my hand."

"Look, there's Eaton's Neck Lighthouse. You're heading out onto Long Island Sound!"

I dropped a little lower to get my bearings. By then the fog was lifting and I could see there was something to his point. Either I'd crossed to the north coast of the island, or our compass was acting up.

"Now we're just above my estate!"

"Most impressive."

And it was. It included a giant castle of crenellated walls, turrets, and towers, along with six or seven smaller buildings, tennis courts, a swimming pool, and a lawn you could easily use as an airstrip. And it was all lavishly illuminated, for no other reason, I suppose, than to impress the less-well-off neighbors.

II

We finally arrived at Rockaway about ten. Just as I'd hoped, the junior officer on watch was easily bluffed into allowing us to land. Nevertheless, he exiled Wilbur to the far end of the field.

I telephoned Rutledge and arranged to meet him at the Plaza for a late supper. The crew still had several cases of Scotch with which to entertain themselves, so I left them in the care of the CPO and brought Congdon into New York with me.

He invited me to spend the night at his estate, but I opted for the hotel. One never knows what sort of adventure might transpire in Manhattan. While he went to meet Rutledge in the Oak Lounge, I checked in.

"Your name?"

"Congdon. Noyes Congdon."

"Oh, Mr. Congdon. It's a privilege to have you stay with us. I'm afraid the only suite available is a smaller one."

"Well, I'm not demanding."

Once handed my key, I turned to find myself entangled with a filly of rare form. And so far, I'd only handled her hindquarters.

"Oh!" she chirped, then spun around to face me. The pirouette was practiced; during it, her abbreviated skirt levitated, allowing a glimpse of two shapely thighs and a strategically positioned lace undergarment.

"Well, I'll be damned," she whispered. "What are you doing here?"

It was Kate. And she was looking especially smart.

"I might ask you the same."

"Me? Fishing.... I figure the next guy may as well be a rich one. No harm in that, is there?"

"Not that I can detect."

"Say, are you here with those swells you traveled to Washington with? What's that younger fella look like? Didn't you tell me he was worth millions?"

"Uh-uh. That lobster's already spoken for."

"Listen, until he's been tossed in the pot, he's on the menu."

"Forget it, kid. You'd be queering my set-up. Look, I'll make it up to you later. I finagled a suite. What's your room number? I'll give you a call."

"Forget it, *chump*. I only give that out to friends."

She stomped off across the lobby and I went into the lounge to join my patrons. Once we'd ordered, Rutledge insisted I provide an update on the mission's status. I painted it as rosy as possible, but with little help from Congdon.

"Why in God's name is this moving so slowly?" the old man demanded. "Maybe I should have just gone along with the Navy."

"I had a ship to prepare, and a crew to train. But don't worry. Just a couple of details to nail down, and we'll be out over the Atlantic in a day or two."

Our food arrived, and a few seconds after that, Kate did as well. She made a show of having come upon me unexpectedly. Before I could stop him, the waiter brought another chair to the table. He placed it opposite Congdon, but Kate complained about the lighting and got

Rutledge to switch places with her. She'd been in double harness since I'd met her, but apparently still remembered how to cut and weave her way through the early turns.

Nevertheless, I felt reasonably confident she'd fade down the home stretch. Congdon's devotion to his Dulcinea seemed absolute. During our trip north, he'd moved on from couplets to sonnets and had written over a dozen of the mawkish tributes. All rather tame, and extremely limited in their imagery. Line after line about Lizzie's becoming nature, hair, lips, and eyes. But strangely—and, I might add, inauspiciously for their wedding night—nothing below the neckline.

He'd just lifted a plump Little Neck clam, nicely balanced on its half shell, when Kate put a hand on his knee. He shuddered and the detached jelly went down his shirtfront. She was upon him with a wet napkin before he even knew what'd happened.

Rutledge was giving me the evil eye. No doubt he assumed I'd brought Kate in to undermine his claim on Congdon's fortune. Had I thought of it earlier, I might well have tried it. But things were complicated enough without taking a chance as risky as that. For a girl who knows what she's about, getting a guy to drop a raw clam down his shirtfront is a soft racket. What would happen later, when his thoughts inevitably drifted back to poor Lizzie, still in the clutches of those diabolical pirates? Whatever his faults, Congdon didn't strike me as fickle.

By now, Rutledge had his heel planted firmly on the toe of my shoe. "Get rid of this uptown floozy or the whole deal's off," he whispered.

I gave him a reassuring nod, then excused myself and went off toward the head. Once out of sight, I flagged down a waiter. Kate had given her maiden name when she'd introduced herself. Now I arranged to have Mrs. Dirk Gilbert paged. A minute later, she joined me by the telephones.

"That ain't playin' fair!" she hissed.

"All's fair in love and cons, sweetie, and this involves plenty of both. There's no way I'll let you muck things up now. But play it my way, and we may be able to work out a deal."

"What sort of deal?"

"I'll do what I can to make sure he picks you over Rutledge's daughter. But only *after* I'm finished with him. I've got twenty-five thousand dollars riding on this."

"How do I know I can trust you?"

"What choice do you have? Besides, you need a divorce before you can nail him to your cross. You'll have to string him along for six months at least, assuming you head to Reno tomorrow."

"I figured if I find the right guy, he'll finance all that."

"With someone like Congdon, you'll need to sink the hook but good."

"Yeah? And how do you propose I do that?"

"You'll need a play as good as the other girl's. Hell, she's been abducted by pirates! Do you think he could abandon her after that?"

"So what do I do? Get abducted by pirates, too?"

"Not what I had in mind, but I suppose that could work.... Take some finesse. And costuming.... Yes, it just might work...."

"What are you talking about?"

"Your abduction. All right, here's the plan: I'll send Rutledge home. Then you come back to the table and I'll leave you alone with Congdon. Lay on some sob story. Confess you're married to a man who beats you. You've found out he's headed here and need to get out of town quick. Congdon has an estate out on Long Island. Get him to take you there."

"That shouldn't be any problem...."

"Then—"

"Oh, I'll know what to do then...."

"Nix that. Overdo the vamping and you'll scare him off. You just get him to take you to the estate. Leave your luggage here, we can call for it tomorrow. Now stay out of sight until I can get rid of Rutledge."

By the time I returned to the table, Congdon had gone off looking for Kate. Rutledge had finished his meal and lit a cigar.

"Don't worry," I assured him. "I paid the girl off. It's the last we'll see of her. But let's make an early night of it so I can keep your future son-in-law out of trouble."

"All right. But don't forget—my daughter *must* be back in time for the wedding. If you can't do the job, I'll announce the reward in the newspapers."

I just smiled. We both knew there was a good reason he hadn't already done that: he'd talked too much, and now found himself at the mercy of my discretion. And as many of my former acquaintances could tell you, that's a very precarious position to find yourself in.

He crossed paths with Congdon on his way out.

"I didn't see a sign of Kate," the floundering fiancé told me. "I hope she's all right."

No sooner had the words left his mouth than the heart bandit herself reappeared. From his fish-eyed expression, I surmised the hook was already planted.

I excused myself and made a beeline for the cab

stand. It was after two when I reached Rockaway. On rousing the crew, I told them we'd be raiding the estate of a well-connected bootlegger that very night. Cheers all around. For the first time in my life, I felt I'd found my calling.

III

It was the night of the new moon and only the stars provided any natural illumination. But I found it easy enough to cross to the island's north shore and follow the well-lit coast. Soon we spotted the lighthouse, and shortly after, the castle itself.

As we descended to the lawn, the lookout spied two figures in the nearby pool. They were bathing *au naturel.* It seemed Congdon's thoughts had yet to drift back to poor Lizzie, still in the clutches of those diabolical pirates.

As the raiding party disembarked—all masked, and garbed as colorfully as we could muster on such short notice—I reminded the men to remain silent, and, as nearly as possible, to run like girls. The results fell well short of the graceful movements of the pirates aboard the *Paris,* but were no doubt peculiar enough to elicit comment later.

Three of the more diminutive men were dispatched to the pool, with orders to subdue Congdon and retrieve Kate. The rest of the party I sent to storm the castle.

Kate was brought to me half-dressed and shivering. I lent her my jacket.

"A little chilly for a swim, isn't it?"

"Once I turned blue, I figured I could count on his gallantry to revive me. You interrupted things. Why didn't you tell me what you had in mind?"

"I thought I had. How's your host?"

"Your hooligans knocked him out cold."

"Good. Consider yourself abducted."

"OK. What now?"

"We make for Rockaway, then in the morning I take you someplace to hide out."

I felt a little bad for undermining her play for Congdon, and for deceiving her about helping her later. But I'd laid my claim first and she was more than capable of finding a replacement.

It didn't take long before the crew realized this abode belonged not to a bootlegger, but rather to that rarest of Jazz Age beings, a bona fide teetotaler. They'd found only three cases of assorted wines in Congdon's huge cellar and two bottles of cooking sherry in his kitchen. Plus a half-quart of gin the scullery maid kept hidden in her mattress. What little of this hadn't been instantly consumed was now loaded onto Wilbur—along with Kate, a leg of lamb, about a hundred and fifty pounds in sterling tableware, and a like amount in scullery maid.

It's generally considered a bad idea to bring a woman aboard ship. But this maid was not just game, she was downright enthusiastic. And having brought Kate along, I wasn't really in a position to quibble. Cinching the deal, Dorie—as the maid was called—seemed to have a calming influence on Albertson, the thrasher of ships' officers.

The sun had crested the horizon when we reached base, and by then I'd come up with a plan for Kate. I took her to my cousin Emmie's place. She and her husband had a roomy apartment not far away in Brooklyn. I'd spent more than a few nights there myself, usually when likewise on the lam.

Thankfully, the husband was away. Emmie herself was a good sixteen years older than me, and he older still. Whether that accounted for why he never took to me, I can't say. But when I was eleven or twelve, and living with my aunt, Emmie's mother, he was always offering me bribes to run away from home. A queer case, all right. But to tell the truth, she was no pillar of sanity herself.

She greeted me now with her customary skepticism.

"I haven't time to explain it all, really. But certainly you've heard about Sesbania?"

"Yes, I have. I always knew it was a mistake to introduce you two. I warned her you were trouble."

"Surely you don't believe I had something to do with her abduction?"

She made a disparaging noise. That woman had more noises at her disposal than the collective inmates of the Central Park Zoo.

"Is this her replacement?"

Kate, who had been standing in the shadows, embarrassed, now showed herself. She was dressed haphazardly, in one of my old suits. There were tears running down her cheeks. Yes, she was *that* good.

"Don't be absurd. This poor girl is Kate. On the run from her brutish husband. She needs a place to hide out for a few days, until she can make arrangements for traveling to Reno." I fed Cousin Emmie a fairy tale worthy of the brothers Grimm—only to have her conclude I'd been responsible for breaking up the couple's happy home. Which brought her back to the subject of Sesbania's predicament and her suspicion I was behind it.

Why is it so many women have a problem with trust? Especially the women I find myself attracted to. (In all honesty, I'd once had an enormous crush on

Emmie, from the age of about six until she went completely off her rocker several years later.)

"I tell you I had nothing to do with it! It happened just as you've heard. Pirates descending from an airship. A very singular airship. In fact, it was something like one of your creations."

"What do you mean, *my creations?*"

"Those ridiculous steam-powered airships of yours."

"*I've told you before*. None of it is of *my* making."

This was rather a sore point with Emmie. For most of my life, she'd been telling stories of visiting airships. At first, they were big and silent. Later, they came to be steam-powered. She claimed they brought her various written archives on which she had based a series of bizarre novels. For twenty years, she'd been expecting these nonsensical books to bring about her imminent literary stardom. They say hope springs eternal. But in her case, willful delusion was nearer the mark.

In order to buttress my defense, I gave her a more detailed account of the affair aboard the *Paris*.

"A calliope? Are you sure?"

"Sounded like it."

"And you think the boarders were all women?"

"Had that appearance."

"Oh, dear."

She went off and returned a minute later with a handwritten manuscript. She located a specific page and placed it before me. It seemed to be an account of a steam-powered airship manned by women.

"So far, the only crossing over has been to provide me with these manuscripts. I never dreamed something like this would happen...."

"Crossing over? Are you saying an airship of fictional Amazons crossed over from your make-believe world and abducted my wife?"

"Well, I think we need to entertain the possibility. Don't you?"

What troubled me most, hers was the first logical explanation I'd heard. I don't mean reasonable—it was far from that. But it *was* logical. It accounted for the only two truly distinctive bits of evidence we had: the female pirates and the steam-powered airship. Everything else— the filigreed daggers, the French perfume, etc.—could be explained any number of ways.

"Assuming I agree—and I'm not saying I do—how do I get her back? Cross over to the fictional world?"

"I wish you'd stop calling it *fictional,* and *make-believe.* But to answer your question, yes. You'll need to do just that."

"How?"

Kate had so far seemed lost by the conversation. Now, however, she entered into the spirit of the thing.

"In *The Wizard of Oz*, Dorothy does it by passing through a storm," she reminded us.

"Yes," Emmie agreed. "There may be something in that."

I began to suspect the two of them were somehow related. If I remember right, both had Irish fathers who drank heavily. Though I suppose that could be mere coincidence.

"Do you honestly think I would steer a patched-up airship—filled with highly combustible hydrogen— directly into a storm?" I asked them both. "That would be the height of insanity!"

It would be, of course. And yet I doubt it will surprise you that two days later I was doing just that.

In the meantime, however, there were preparations to be made. I arrived back at Rockaway to find Congdon waiting for me. He looked rather agitated.

"They've taken her as well!" He handed me a morning paper. The front-page account wasn't lacking in details—and downright candid in regards to the early-morning swim. Evidently, his staff had been in a talkative mood. "How will I explain this to Lizzie?"

"I wouldn't worry about that. Once you've rescued her from those fiendish pirates, I doubt she'll waste time itemizing your petty indiscretions."

"Yes, I suppose. But Kate will be there as well.... You know, the coincidence... It seems rather remarkable, doesn't it?"

"It is a bit strange, but so is everything else about this affair. We just need to take things as they come. At least this time we're prepared. We set sail on the morrow."

"The sooner the better. I have a nagging fear I might meet another girl, and then..."

"Yes, better we leave before that happens. First though, we need to supply the ship. And we may need something to bargain with when we meet up with those pirates. Something they're likely to value equally."

"You aren't suggesting we give them other women as replacements?"

"That's a thought, but I was speaking of gold. Pirates generally have a soft spot for treasure, and only in the rarest of circumstances do they accept checks. Take three men with you and get a couple thousand half eagles.... And then stop by Tiffany's for the same amount in jewels—diamonds, preferably."

"All right, but do you have three men we can trust?"

"Good point. Use your chauffeur."

He left and I turned to the task of refitting the ship. The envelope was filled and as a reserve three dozen extra tanks of hydrogen were stowed aboard. As was an extra supply of gasoline. A dangerous mixture, to be sure. Particularly for a ship its crew had already come to call the Flying Coffin. However, there was no way of knowing how easily these could be procured in a world conjured by the mind of Cousin Emmie.

All this didn't leave much room for rations. But with luck, we'd be able to live off the land—assuming there'd be something resembling land as we knew it.

CHAPTER 5.

HOLEY BOOKS BEGET NOBLE ACTS

Aggie Ready showed up about seven that evening. I'd forgotten that little nuisance.

"A pirate raid on Long Island! Jeez, ain't you somethin'? Thinkin' you could pull the same stunt again.... And in my own back yard!"

"That's a very serious allegation. And completely unfounded."

"The *real* story'll be on page one of the mornin' edition."

"There is such a thing as libel, you know."

"Ha!" she said. "Not in your case, there ain't."

"I hope you don't stoop to using double negatives like that in your writing."

Wrong tack. Her eyes narrowed and her manner took on a menacing quality.

"Where's Congdon? I want to see what he has to say to *this*." She displayed a seaman's canvas cap, the ubiquitous Dixie cup.

"Oh, come on. There must be ten thousand sailors in and around New York."

"Yeah? And how many with a name like Ropheas Albertson?" She inverted the hat so I could see the name written in laundry marker.

There was no arguing the point. It was a unique name, all right. What's more, I suspected his parents' unfortunate choice at least partly accounted for the man's disposition.

I needed to get rid of this provoking rib before

Congdon returned from his errands. I grabbed her by the arm and pulled her toward the guardhouse. She objected with both feet, her free arm, and a vocabulary worthy of a tall-water sailor. In order to restrict her movements, I picked her up and slung her over a shoulder. Now she pulled up my shirttail and ran a nail across my back. I still bear the scar today. Try explaining that to the little woman.

I flopped her down at the feet of the guards. "What do you mean allowing a newspaperwoman onto the field like this?"

"She had an OK from the press office."

"Clearly forged. The woman is a... a Red sympathizer. An agitator."

"Why, you—! ...Don't listen to him, boys!"

"Take her to the brig at once. Tomorrow she can make her case to the CO." They hesitated. *"That's an order!"*

As they took hold of her arms, I grabbed Albertson's hat. "Government property."

The moment Congdon returned, I handed out two-hour passes to the crew—just enough time for them to visit the blind pig up the beach, but not enough to become completely blotto. Once they were gone from sight, he and I loaded the gold and jewels aboard. Then we began hollowing out his traveling library of romantic poesy. He objected at first, but had to admit there was no place less likely to be searched by the crew.

"But not the rhyming dictionary! Here, take the Swinburne. A little too indelicate for my blood."

Congdon had his finer points—several million, in fact—but I'd had all I could take of the insipid bromide's company. Once we'd finished concealing the goods, I suggested he spend a final night at his castle. Then I borrowed a staff car and stopped by Cousin Emmie's to make my farewells.

"I'd like to see you get out of this one." Husband Harry had returned, and it was he who greeted me at the door.

"I'm not sure what you're talking about."

"Uh-huh."

We went into the dining room, where Kate and Emmie were seated at the table. Kate looked uncharacteristically miserable. She'd been crying, and this time it wasn't an act.

Emmie looked up at me. "You bastard." It was the only time I'd heard her swear, and God knows I'd given plenty of cause previously. "Come on, Harry. We better let them talk."

I sat down next to Kate. "What did you tell them?"

"I'm anticipating."

"Anticipating what?"

"*What the hell do you think?*"

"Oh. And you told them it's mine?"

"No—I got sick this morning, and your cousin guessed why. So I admitted it. They both leapt to the conclusion it was you."

"Did you know about it before coming to New York?"

"Suspected."

"That's why you were playing so hard for Congdon?"

"I thought maybe if I acted fast enough, I could convince him it was his."

"If we hadn't interrupted things poolside?"

She shrugged.

"Have you thought about going back to Dirk?"

"Not seriously. I couldn't bear that now. No, I'll deal with it, one way or another.... And don't worry, I'll explain things to your cousin."

"Pack your bags."

"For where?"

"Long Island."

"Are you serious?"

"He's home. And this time no one will louse up your game. You might even make something of him."

"I like the little lug. He's goofy. Dirk was never goofy. But what about his girl, Lizzie?"

"Odds are, it wasn't so much her being soft on Congdon as her father being soft on his fortune."

"What about your twenty-five thousand?"

"What's money, where a friend's happiness is concerned?"

She gave me a curious look, then put a hand to my forehead.

Noble acts come easily to me. Or, I should say, acting noble comes easily. I'd already decided to leave Congdon behind—which is why I'd suggested he spend the night at his estate. Handing him off to Kate meant forgoing the twenty-five thousand Rutledge had promised. But the twenty thousand in gold and jewels hidden in Congdon's traveling library would soften the blow. And that was a sure thing. Not just the promise of a blister who'd sell his own daughter to save his skin.

On dropping off Kate, I gave her a few final words of advice.

"Get him out of town tomorrow. And travel incognito. It will be better if Rutledge doesn't find out we've put the kibosh on his plan until I get back."

"OK. From what I hear, Reno's very pleasant this

time of year." She gave me a peck on the cheek. "Good luck."

"Thanks, I'll need it."

II

It was two by the time I returned to Rockaway, and another hour before the last of the crew made it aboard. They were feeling no pain. But there wasn't a man among them not able to stand, and I took that as an auspicious sign. Better still, Dorie had failed to return with them. She was a girl who spread her favors widely, and the jealousies had already taken a toll. The prohibition against women was a sound one.

"Prepare to make way, Mr. Cartwright."

The CPO gave me a smart salute, then promptly fell flat on his back. He was quickly removed to his berth and his place taken by Dombrowski—as able a sailor as any on board, though currently looking a little worse for wear. One eye had swollen shut and his nose seemed to have a new crease to it. I learned later that he'd tempted Dorie from Albertson, who subsequently made his objections known via a balled fist. At last report, the randy maid had eloped with the man delivering ice to the officers' mess.

Luckily, the night was a calm one and none of us were put to the test. We ascended to eight hundred feet and headed out over the Atlantic. All sorts of vessels plied the sea below us—trawlers, coasters, tramp steamers, even a liner or two—and certain elements among the crew were already lobbying for a chance at the promised booty. I dropped down to five hundred feet as we passed Montauk. About fifteen miles to the east there was a rise in the sea floor. A perfect place for a rum-runner's ship to drop anchor.

There were three of them, lying about a thousand yards apart. We doused our lights and dropped down another three hundred feet. I thought I'd replicate the approach we'd used with so much success off of Charleston. Sadly, these rum-runners were not so benign.

"Holy hell!" cried Blight, expressing feelings shared by us all at that moment. "The sons-of-bitches got machine guns mounted!"

No doubt, the competitiveness of the New York marketplace necessitated a greater preparedness. I quickly took the ship to five thousand feet and so out of their range. This was above our pressure height, which meant we needed to vent some precious hydrogen to keep the envelope from overexpanding in the lower pressures surrounding it. But safety first.

Once we'd reached that height, I found a steady airstream blowing in our favor, and, since the gas had already been lost, decided to remain there. I suggested to the crew that we take turns getting some rest. Their pirate appetites sated for the time being, they agreed.

A secondary cost of flying at higher altitudes is the drop in cabin temperature. At five thousand feet, the temperature is almost twenty degrees lower than at sea level. My quarters were just off the control room and I went in to retrieve my flight jacket.

The cabin was tiny by any measure—a chair, a little desk beneath a small porthole, a locker, and a bunk barely long enough to stretch out on. Above and below was space now taken up with ship's stores. It took my eyes a moment to adjust to the relative dimness. When they did, I noticed someone dressed in a sailor's whites inhabiting my bunk. I was about to admonish the man when certain incongruities came to my attention. Most prominently, the overlarge and sloppily lipsticked mouth. My guest was none other than Augusta Ready.

"How in God's name did you get aboard? And where'd you get that uniform?"

"They left me guarded by a pipsqueak disinclined to hit a dame until it was too late."

"Well, I don't know what you have in mind...."

"I'm gettin' to the bottom of this—once and for all." She pulled a pack of cigarettes out of her leather pouch and stuck one in her mouth, then uncovered a book of matches.

"I'd think twice before lighting that."

She struck a match. "Why?"

"Well, for one thing, those tanks up above your head are filled with hydrogen."

She lit her cigarette and blew out the match with a skeptical "Ha."

"Listen, I'm not joking...."

"The Navy stopped using hydrogen over a year ago. I wrote about it myself."

"True. But this ship is a special case. Anyway, if you don't believe in the hydrogen, there's also thirty gallons of gasoline situated just beneath you."

She bent her head down and inspected the canisters under the bunk. But only after taking another long drag did she crush out the cigarette.

"Say, why's it gettin' so cold?"

"We're a mile up. You'll be needing something to keep you warm...."

"Not a chance, bub...."

I took a wool union suit out of the locker and tossed

it to her. "I was thinking more on the lines of this. Better put it on now, and wrap yourself up. I'll come back with a flight outfit later. And don't leave the cabin."

"I'll go where I want!"

"Suit yourself, but the crew isn't in the best of moods. Especially where women are concerned."

When Cartwright recovered consciousness a few hours later, I left him in charge and went in to check on Aggie. She sat bundled up under a pile of blankets and the last of my clean laundry, only her eyes and nose visible.

"How's my little stowaway?"

"If she don't get to a piss-pot soon, someone's gonna need a change of sheets."

"Sorry, not now. Too many of the boys out there. Here." I tossed her a mason jar I kept handy for emergencies. It landed on the bunk beside her and she peered down at it without moving.

"This a joke?"

"No, no joke. I'll be in the bunk next door; Mr. Congdon wasn't able to make the trip. If you need me for anything else, rap on the partition."

"I won't need you."

She was a disagreeable creature, all right. And her assumption that any man setting eyes on her couldn't wait to bed her bordered on the comical. And yet... I found myself thinking thoughts....

You see, I've had a weakness for disagreeable women dating back to my Latin teacher. There is, however, a key difference between the two types. My old instructress was sincerely cold and uncaring, always far more demanding than accommodating. Aggie, on the other hand, would have me believe she had no use for men at all. But it was all a little too theatrical. The practiced dismissiveness, and the affected language and costume. No, she wasn't the cynic she made herself out to be. It was simply that she equated sentiment with weakness.

There was no doubt in my mind that given just one night, I could have her purring like a kitten. But then what? When girls like her fall, they fall hard. And it would be that suffocatingly romantic strain of the disease. She may as well have hung a sign around her neck: "No Returns Accepted."

Once in Congdon's cabin, I checked a few of the books to make sure the booty hadn't been discovered. It was all there. Reassured, I fell asleep with Swinburne's weighty tome beneath my pillow.

It was nearly six when I relieved Cartwright, the sun already above the horizon.

"Any idea of our position?" I asked.

"Middle of the ocean someplace."

For the average seaman, navigation was a complete riddle. While he went off to his berth, I took out the sextant and made some calculations. We were 500 miles due east of Montauk, give or take, and traveling at something in the range of seventy-five knots. The wind being at our back made all the difference.

I set us on a heading of sixty degrees east-northeast. In ten hours we'd be about where the S.S. *Paris* had been when the pirates boarded. There was no particular reason to think the pirate ship would be in the same position, it just seemed as good a place to start as any.

The crew remained largely ignorant about the true nature of our assignment. But there'd be no chance of hiding it now that we were so far from the coast. Once they'd all had their share of bunk time, I assembled the men in the control room.

"I imagine you're all wondering about our mission."

"You said we were going after rum-runners," Dombrowski noted.

"Yes. But we've another, much more vital task than that. We're hunting for pirates. The pirates who kidnapped those pitiful women from the steamship S.S. *Paris*."

"I thought *we* were piratin'?" Albertson conjectured.

"No, we're more like privateers."

"What's the difference?"

"Plenty. And the distinction is critically important. You see, we're sanctioned by the government, on a most noble mission: to keep American womanhood safe. Many great national heroes started out as privateers. Take Sir Francis Drake..."

"Who the hell is he?"

"Saved England from the Spanish—*and* got fabulously rich in the process."

"Pirates can get fabulously rich...."

"Yes, but at the end of the day, the pirate is sent to the gallows, where his rotting corpse is left hanging as a warning to others. Meanwhile, the privateer has taverns, thoroughfares, and public high schools named in his honor. Best of all, this veneer of legitimacy comes at almost no cost whatsoever."

"We still get to take on the rum-runners?"

"To our hearts' content! In fact, it's encouraged. We just need to throw a heroic deed into the mix every now and then. And that's where the rescue of these damsels in distress comes in."

"And so once we rescue these damsels, it's back to pirating rum-runners?"

"Exactly."

"And do we get to keep any of this American womanhood safe for ourselves?"

"That might tend to dull the heroic sheen a little. But I'll tell you what: if any of these paragons of virtue strike your fancy, you're free to make an offer. And if she accepts, consider her yours."

"And it won't cut into our share of the loot?"

"No, she'll be frosting on the cake. So what do you say?"

They said little. So I broke out the half-case of Scotch I'd hidden aboard. This got me a slim majority, but Albertson and a couple other bruisers were making for a vocal minority.

"Ain't these pirates got guns?"

"Just knives, from what I saw. And besides..."

"And besides what?"

"Well, I hadn't wanted to mention it, in case it would make subduing them seem unmanly...."

"Go on!"

"These airship pirates... I believe they're women."

"What about *them?*"

"What do you mean?"

"Well, can we keep them?"

"You know, that's an interesting question. I rather doubt the law of admiralty touches on it. But I don't see why not."

Cheers all around.

At lunch time, I brought Aggie a plate of sandwiches along with Congdon's flight jacket. She sat huddled in a corner of the bunk reading.

"Jeez, what a nutty book."

She'd chosen from my locker Cousin Emmie's first novel.

"Someday I'll introduce you to the author and that will explain everything."

"Is it true Walt Whitman referred to his thing as a pond snipe?"

"I can't attest to it personally, but Cousin Emmie prides herself on her literary prowess."

She peered out the little porthole. "So where are we now?"

"Near the Grand Banks, south of Newfoundland."

"You expect to find rum-runners way out here?"

"I told you before, I'm going after those airship pirates. And the crew is with me."

"You could convince those jackshites of just about anythin'. I ain't so gullible. How long ya gonna keep me a prisoner in here?"

"Leave anytime you want. But be forewarned: the crew has had its liquor ration and is in a celebratory mood."

She picked up her book and I discreetly took away her mason jar. One hesitates to embarrass a lady, but I doubt many of the crew could have filled it so completely. After a careful trip to the head, I went into Congdon's cabin for another four-hour nap. Swinburne lay right where I'd left him.

Early that evening, I emerged to find Wilbur traveling in circles and the crew in desperate need of diversion. The word mutiny was being bandied about with an unnerving casualness.

III

Once again I assembled the men. First, I reminded them that I was the only one aboard with the skills required to navigate a ship. This impressed them far less than you might imagine.

Next, I suggested we draw up articles. "This way you can be sure the ship is run in a fair manner."

I'd hoped to be able to control the process. But they were better schooled in the business than I'd expected.

"All right," Blight agreed. "Article One: When we spot a ship, in the air or in the sea, a vote will be taken as to whether we attack said ship. How say ye?"

I had here that most troublesome of seamen, the fo'c'sle lawyer. His proposal carried, as did those that followed:

Article Two: All men, regardless of rank, will receive an equal share in all prizes.

Article Three: If any man keep booty hidden from the company, he shall be marooned with one bottle of water and a pistol.

We didn't have a chance to hear Article Four, as the lookout interrupted with the announcement that he'd spotted a ship two miles off our starboard bow. The vote to attack was unanimous—at the last minute, I decided I'd better throw in with the majority so I could go with the boarders and perhaps minimize the carnage.

Having so recently met resistance off Long Island, we approached cautiously. This boat flew a Norwegian ensign, and looked distinctly like a fishing trawler. But the crew reasoned it was mere subterfuge and that the blond men waving to us from the deck below were simply feigning affability.

The first of our party were lowered down with submachine guns blazing. When the men who'd waved us greetings disappeared below deck, the gunners followed. One by one, they were rendered unconscious by the canny occupants of the trawler. Five more of us had arrived on deck by then, but the fishermen, now armed with the Thompsons, quickly had us subdued.

The Norwegians seemed more shocked by our aggression than angry. And we had little trouble coming to terms with them. We handed over what cash we had on our persons—just shy of three hundred dollars, all told— plus the machine guns, my watch, and a seaman named Peckham. (They'd held impromptu auditions and determined he was the only one among us with a singing voice, a bass, which they happened to need for an upcoming fishermen's choir competition.)

In return, they gave us our freedom, a barrel of haddock, and a parrot named Knut who refused to converse in Norwegian. When we returned to Wilbur and explained the outcome to those who'd remained behind, a certain disagreeableness took hold. One no amount of haddock was likely to mollify. I felt obliged to dispense the bottle of rare vintage brandy I'd been saving for my reunion with Sesbania—the last drop of liquor on board.

As night descended, I sent the majority of the men to their quarters and took us up to a comfortable two thousand feet. By now we were at the approximate latitude, but still a few hours shy of the point of contact. I changed our heading to due east. Outside of some cloud activity to our south, the sky was clear and the stars out in abundance.

Our normal range would have only just allowed us to reach our objective before needing to immediately turn around for home. Which is why I'd loaded all the extra fuel. By using the engines only as necessary, I hoped we could hold that position for several days.

"I can maintain course all right," I told the others in

the control room. "You men go start transferring the extra gasoline to the main fuel tanks. And remember: safety is our watchword."

I'd forgotten to return Aggie's mason jar and suspected her circumstances might have become dire.

"You can come out now. The lady's *toilette*, if you need it, is just this way."

She bolted for it, but stopped dead on opening the door.

"Jesus H. Christ! Who the hell's been pissin' in here? Elephants?"

"You're lucky it isn't worse—we've only been out a day. And better keep your voice down."

She closed the door on herself, muttering, and the parrot, which had so far been mute, took up her refrain: "*Jesus H. Christ! Who the hell's been pissin' in here? Elephants?*"

After seven iterations, I tried silencing him with the sharp end of the sextant.

It was then that events took a turn for the strange—or perhaps I should say, a turn for the stranger. First, the airstream which had been so favorable abruptly reversed. We were barely making twenty knots. I tried dropping lower, but with no improvement. So then I took us up to four thousand feet. Then five thousand, and finally six thousand—as high as I dared go. But there wasn't a favorable wind at any altitude.

I could see the disturbance responsible just a few miles off to the south. Remembering Kate's suggestion that transit into the world of make-believe might require heading into a storm, I debated whether to seize the initiative. As tempests go, this one looked fairly restrained—a mere squall. With luck, it would be a quick passage to the other side. I steered straight for it.

Soon, however, powerful winds rendered the controls inoperative. I vented more hydrogen to bring us down. But an updraft pushed us back heavenward. Only then did I realize what we were up against. It was a hurricane. About two months too early, and two thousand miles north of normal.

Wilbur went into a wide counterclockwise spin. The sky and sea were impossible to distinguish from one another, and the compass, altimeter, and weather instruments were either inoperative or giving out impossible readings.

Then I smelled gasoline. The men had been knocked off their feet while transferring it. Aggie tumbled out of the head and, from her expression, I surmised she was not feeling her best. I escorted her back to my cabin and strapped her to the bunk with my dress belt. For once, she made no protest. But the damned parrot wouldn't shut up.

"We're sinkin', Captain! Davy Jones is callin' us home! Women and parrots to the boats!"

By now, the entire crew had been roused. I assured them there was nothing to worry about and that I'd been through many worse storms before. All nonsense, of course. Then Blight unhelpfully brought up the occasion when I mistook fireworks for a thunderstorm and in my caution brought my ship down in the middle of a Fourth of July celebration in Central Park. Normally this might at least have amused the crew, but not at this particular juncture. And not with the pestilent parrot squawking about imminent death.

Now, with a jolt, the ship began to spin in the opposite direction. Though no vote was taken, I think there was a general consensus among us that one of the failures of airship design is that there's no railing over which to get sick. Even the parrot was reduced to emitting inarticulate groans.

On and on we spun, for what seemed like hours. Then—just as I began having serious doubts about Wilbur's integrity—stillness. We were in the eye. Gradually, we regained our footing and began assessing the damage. It could hardly have been worse. The engines were out, the rudder disabled, the envelope seemed to be leaking, and there wasn't a single drop of liquor with which to placate the crew. Or me, for that matter.

With conditions so quiet, I went by my cabin to check on Aggie; there she was, sleeping like a baby.

"Look!" someone shouted.

A whale shark flashed by our port side. Then off the starboard, a giant ray glided back toward the ocean below, while vast ribbons of kelp drifted down from the heavens. It went on like that for twelve long hours— raging storm all around us, but a heartening calmness in our immediate vicinity.

However, the battering we'd received earlier had taken a toll: we were slowly losing altitude. I had the men break out several of our spare tanks of hydrogen and release them into Wilbur's giant envelope. This slowed our descent, but only with a constant injection of gas. And now the ship was infused with the fumes of spilt gasoline and leaking hydrogen. Any stray spark, even the merest bit of static electricity, and we'd be meeting our maker.

And yet, through it all, Aggie slept on.

Chapter 6.

Sure Ain't Kansas

Wilbur hit the ground with a dull thud.

I'd just pulled myself up off the floor when Aggie opened the cabin door.

"Hey, what's going on?"

The men—at least those still conscious—looked on her quizzically.

"This is Petty Officer Redfern," I told them. "On a secret assignment for the Navy Department." By then the lipstick had mostly disappeared, and between the uniform and Aggie's raspy voice it seemed conceivable they'd accept her as just a diminutive seaman with a non-regulation haircut. Conceivable, perhaps, but well short of probable.

"Petty officer, my bunghole!" Albertson opined. "He's got himself a cabin boy!"

His comment incited a hearty round of laughter at my expense. Nonetheless, I decided to let his misclassification of gender stand. Were those reprobates to learn the truth, the odds of protecting whatever remained of the girl's virtue would have been less than slim. As Aggie retreated back into the cabin—and the parrot repeated, *"He's got himself a cabin boy!"* several times in succession—I led the men outside.

We'd landed on a wide sandy beach. But I found it impossible to determine our geographical location with any precision. Although the compass was now working, the ship's chronometer had stopped—and my watch was strapped to the wrist of a Norwegian fisherman. However, given how warm it felt, and the tropical foliage which surrounded us, I estimated that we were far to the south of where we had first encountered the cyclone. And from the angle of the sun, the time about eleven in the morning.

There were two men still unconscious, but for the rest of us it was mostly a matter of cuts and bruises. While these were tended to, the CPO and I looked over Wilbur. The ship leaned to port at about 30 degrees, and the propellers on that side had all been bent. The keel and rudder, however, were miraculously intact. And though the envelope was once again flaccid, Cartwright was confident the tears could be repaired.

A brief survey of our surroundings revealed no signs of civilization. Had we chanced upon a desert island? A distinct possibility—they did still exist, after all—but one I thought wise to keep to myself. I feared the prospect might unnerve the crew, and most particularly our lone female.

Two men were sent in opposite directions down the beach to act as lookouts.

"Go down at least a mile. And take the flare guns. If you see someone approaching us, let one loose."

Next I sent the balance of the crew out to conduct a more extensive reconnaissance of the area.

"We don't know who or what we might be dealing with, so be cautious. Under no circumstances act the aggressor." As an extra safety measure, I declined to issue the men arms. We were going to need help to get out of this predicament and shooting up the natives would almost certainly make negotiations difficult. I wasn't anxious to die on some foreign beach like Captain Cook and so many others.

I was alone now with the two men still unconscious and Aggie, who'd just emerged from the cabin.

"Any snakes out there?"

"None that I noticed."

"I've got to... you know."

"Wait." I went in and found her a copy of *Capt. Billy's Whiz Bang*. "Serves as reading material, too."

The moment she disappeared into the scrub, I began hauling Congdon's poetry collection down a path that ran oblique to hers. It took three trips, including one to fetch the trenching tool. Digging was no problem, as the soil was all sand. But no sooner would I go down a couple feet than the sides would collapse. Two feet it would have to be. I laid the books containing the jewels in the hole and refilled it, then spread some dead foliage about to obscure it.

Twenty paces due south, I dug a second hole. In this one, I placed the books containing the gold half eagles. Having once made the mistake of placing all my treasure in one place (i.e., Sesbania's midsection), I was determined not to make it again. On refilling this second hole, I paced the distance from the beach, and then from a nearby sinkhole having a suggestive contour. It was strikingly reminiscent of the anatomical feature Walt Whitman called his pond snipe, and we men of the naval air arm refer to as our mooring mast. Just as I finished recording my map on a scrap of paper, a flare shot up into the sky. Someone was approaching the ship.

By the time I got back, one of the wounded men— the Italian, Dombrowski—had regained consciousness and waded out to a fishing smack just off the beach. In it were three black men, one of whom wore a suit and clerical collar.

"Says he's a Reverend Somebody," Dombrowski told me.

"Reverend Sweeting," the visitor explained. "What a fascinating craft. Does it actually fly?"

"It did, before we tangled with that hurricane," I told him.

"Hurricane?"

"Well, cyclone of some sort. Where are we, by the way?"

"Andros Island..."

"Ah... And where exactly is that?"

"The Bahamas!"

"We were blown a little off course, it seems. Is there a town nearby?"

"A village, not too far down the beach. I myself am over from New Providence—I come for Sunday services."

"Is that Nassau?"

"That's right."

"Two of my crew were injured in the crash. Would you mind transporting them to the hospital there?"

"Not at all."

We'd just gotten the two on board when Aggie called to me from the scrub. I trotted over, but when I neared, she shouted for me to stop.

"I was takin' a bath in a spring when some son-of-a-bitch stole my clothes."

Her girlish form was only nominally concealed behind the sparse foliage and a rosy blush. The scene brought to mind a classical painting, the modest maid surprised in the forest by an observer, a satyr more often than not.... Then she opened her mouth and the spell was broken.

"Hey, ya goddamned galoot! Quit staring and get me something to wear!"

I went in to my cabin and brought back a shirt and pants. After tossing the togs over her shrub, I returned to the boat now preparing to make way.

"Would you be willing to take along another passenger, Reverend? A young lady here... Seems to have lost her luggage."

"Not at all."

Aggie emerged looking even less affable than usual, and only too happy to avail herself of the reverend's transport.

"So long, skeezicks," she said to me. "And if I never see you again, it will be jake with me!"

The parrot flew out to the boat and echoed her, "*So long, skeezicks!*"

I waved to Aggie as they left. She replied with a gesture some might consider distinctly unladylike. Gratitude did not number among Miss Ready's more conspicuous qualities. But at least I was rid of the damned parrot.

Another flare shot into the sky; someone was approaching from the opposite direction. Before I learned who, the crew began trickling in. They'd seen no one. I told them about the reverend taking away the injured, but made no mention of Aggie. Whether it had been one of them who'd made off with her things I couldn't discern, and I certainly wasn't going to inquire. With luck, in all the excitement of the crash, they'd forgotten ever having seen her.

A large party of Bahamians arrived from down the beach—twenty or thirty men, women, and children. They seemed fascinated by Wilbur. At his request, I gave the apparent leader of the clan a tour. He listened closely, particularly when I explained the engines.

"We're roasting a pig. Come and join us. I might even be able to rustle up some rum."

He needed say no more. We followed them back to the village, where we were feted like honored guests. It was only some time later, and after a good deal of rum, that I noticed the headman and a number of the other villagers had absented themselves. I located two men of the crew still ambulatory and had them return with me to the ship.

On our arrival, we found a well-organized salvage operation under way. They'd driven several wagons up the beach and were busily filling them with the remaining cans of gasoline, window panes, bits of plumbing, and even a couple tanks of hydrogen. They'd found the engines too heavy to move, but two of their number were disassembling them and making off with the parts.

I wore my ceremonial sword, but we were otherwise weaponless. And though none of them openly displayed arms, I suspected the gun locker topped the list of assets pillaged. To test the matter risked starting a bloodbath. And likely as not, mine would be the first to be spilt. Anyway, as fate would have it, the consequences of their pillaging would be rendered moot soon enough.

The wagons loaded, we all returned to the festivities. And, after sharing another dozen bottles of rum, pledged ourselves to a lifelong friendship. At least, I believe that's what we pledged. With each passing bottle, their patois became more difficult to interpret. It was sometime after midnight that one of the villagers came running from up the beach and announced that an alien party had descended on Wilbur.

A number of us, seamen and villagers, hurried back

to the scene of the crash. A dozen men in uniform and armed with cutlasses were waiting for us on the beach. They'd arrived in a pair of sloops now anchored in the shallows. With them were an equal number of similarly armed but far-less-reputable-looking characters.

These latter birds looked for all the world like pirates. Had the Bahamians come once again under their sway, just as they had in piracy's Golden Age? If we'd crossed over into Cousin Emmie's make-believe world, anything was possible.

They had us sit on the sand with hands clasped behind our heads. Then the chief pirate approached Wilbur with another man carrying a lantern.

"Better leave that behind," I shouted. "You're liable to blow the entire ship to kingdom come."

I meant it as a warning, of course. But I neglected to take into account that there's a certain sort of person who relishes nothing so much as blowing things to kingdom come—just the sort of person you find consorting with pirates. The ruffian with the lantern swung his arm in a couple of loops, then let the lamp loose in the direction of Wilbur's drooping envelope.

The ensuing conflagration was visually spectacular, but it wasn't until the spare tanks of hydrogen began exploding that one could fairly call the results earsplitting. So loud was it, the remainder of the crew—whom we'd left comatose back at the village—revived and came running up the beach. When the fire finally died out, my men and I were crowded onto the sloops and transported to the jail in Nassau.

All in all, my first effort in pursuit of the pirate kidnappers had fallen considerably short of the success I'd anticipated.

II

There was nothing especially gruesome about the Nassau jail, but quarters were cramped—sixteen of us in a cell built to accommodate six. Now suffering the effects of all the rum they'd consumed, the men crowded two and three to a bunk, the unlucky surplus collapsing onto the sticky floor. Fortunately for me, I'd learned to sleep while standing during my long watches at sea.

About eight the next morning, we were given plates of beans and rice. There weren't many takers. I inquired of the jailers if I could have a word with their chief, but their ensuing merriment left me in some doubt that my request would be conveyed to the man in charge.

Two hours later, they began summoning one man at a time for questioning. They were choosing randomly, so I made myself inconspicuous at the back of the cell. Once the first men returned, I hoped to gain some inkling of what we were being charged with and thereby massage my own testimony into as inoffensive a story as possible.

Our captors, however, were either too wily or too brutal to allow any such conference. No men were returned to the cell. The general consensus among the ranks was that since we'd heard no shots fired, they were being hanged by the neck. The next time the jailers came to select a candidate, the whole cell attempted to make themselves inconspicuous.

"I'll go," I said, with all the phony bravado I'd learned to manifest years back at the Academy. Being an optimist, you see, I suspected that the men were simply being forced to sign articles, swearing themselves to a life of piracy. It wasn't my first choice of occupation, but it ranked far ahead of rotting corpse, the likely alternative.

The jailers accepted my offer, but I'd failed to impress the crew.

"Why not you? You're the fool that got us into this."

"Yeah! I'd like to give him the noose myself!"

The one component of naval command I'd never quite got the knack of was maintaining the confidence of the crew. Well, that and seamanship.

They brought me to a bright, sunlit room and seated me at a table opposite three inquisitors: on the right, the pirate chief who'd captured us on the beach; in the center, a portly old duck in a uniform I took to be that of the constabulary; and on the left, a woman in a casual summer dress. She looked to be closing in on forty. Not what you would call a stunner, but attractive in her own way.

"Who are you and for what reason did you invade our colony?" the policeman asked.

"Lieutenant Van Slyke, United States Navy. Commander of the U.S.S...." I'd forgotten Wilbur had never been christened. "The, ah, airship the gentleman at the far end of the table incinerated last night."

The lady bit her cheek. I'd amused her—or so I thought.

"And I assure you, we had no intention of intruding on your fine colony, but were simply carried here in the great storm of the night before."

"We had no storm."

"Well, we encountered it quite a ways to the north. It left the ship immobilized, and I imagine we simply drifted here by chance."

"And what is your ship's mission?"

Here is where I put my foot into it. Without evidence to the contrary, I'd convinced myself that pirates were in control of the place.

"Similar to yours, I imagine. Hunting rum-runners...."

The two men exchanged looks. And the lady turned to look out the window. She was trying to hide her expression. This time I *had* amused her—but not to my advantage.

"So you admit it?" the man I no longer suspected of being a pirate chief asked.

Some quick equivocation seemed in order. It wasn't pirates I was dealing with, but rum-runners. Which was only logical, given the Bahamas' proximity to the Florida coast. I'd let Emmie's romantic fantasy get the better of me.

"Well, those were our orders.... But I never intended..."

"Several of your crewmen say you were wholeheartedly behind it."

"No, no, certainly not. One must follow orders, of course...."

"Were you under orders when you attacked the Tortugas?"

"Oh, yes. A direct order, coming from the Navy Department." Now I could play my strong suit; prevarication comes as easily to me as breathing. "I was told to destroy the stores there. To do otherwise would have meant immediate court-martial."

"Your crew says it was all consumed—on your orders."

"Well, one likes to keep a happy ship...."

"What about the schooner you happened upon off of Charleston?" The woman spoke for the first time. "You couldn't have received any order in advance of attacking that."

"No, not a precise order...."

"And you were flying the same craft which landed on Andros Island?"

"Yes, same ship."

"Powered by?"

"Well, the usual sort of aircraft engines. These were Italian-made."

"But now... gone...." She'd addressed this to the scruffy fellow, but he avoided her gaze by making a survey of his footwear.

"We combed the area this morning," the policeman told her. "Only melted metal and ashes."

"Then I think we've heard enough," she told the others. The lady, it seemed, ruled this roost.

They took me to another part of the jail and locked me in a much smaller cell. It had a single high window and a solid door with only a little hatch to speak through. But the jailers weren't in a speaking mood.

Late that night, I called out, in order to see if any of the others were similarly situated. No one responded. I tried again, louder. This time I attracted the attention of a jailer.

"It ain't no use," he told me. He was an older fellow, not in uniform, and looking somewhat pirate-like. "Ain't no one else about."

"What's happened to the others?"

"Let go."

"Freed? Then why am I..."

"'Cause they all testified *agin* you. Said how they never wanted to steal from anyone, but you made them. 'Til finally they mutinied."

"What filthy liars!"

"All told the same story, I hear."

"Damned conspirators!"

VIRTUE AT MARKET PRICE

My protests seemed to amuse him. I had the uncanny feeling he'd discerned my true character and knew how ironic my situation was.

"Who is it running this place? The rum-runners themselves?"

"That's right. And most here think they're doing a real fine job of it."

"What do they have planned for me?"

"A trial."

He walked back to his lair cackling. I inferred from that my trial was unlikely to follow the normal rules of jurisprudence.

This was confirmed the next morning when the man appointed to defend me arrived for a consultation. He looked about twenty, unusually thin, and of a nervous disposition.

"You *are* a lawyer, aren't you?"

"Lawyer? Well, not per se. Shipping clerk. For Miss Littko."

"Who's Miss Littko?"

"The judge, among other things."

"I see. Would she be the same lady who questioned me yesterday?"

"More than likely."

"And may I assume she has interests smuggling liquor into the U.S.?"

"Well, you won't get anyone to confirm that, not in so many words...."

"Charleston, specifically?"

"Again, there may be rumors...."

"I see. What defense do you plan to present?"

"Defense? Oh, well... I suggest we plead for mercy."

"Otherwise... hanging?"

"Oh, we're not barbarians here. No, no hangings...."

"Thank God for that."

"They give you a half-pint of water and set you adrift in a dinghy."

"Miami's just a couple hundred miles.... And I'm in reasonable shape.... Yes, I think I could make that."

"Oh, sure. Assuming they gave you oars."

"I see. Well, just the same, the current would take me along the seaboard. I'd be bound to encounter a ship plying the coast...."

"I suppose. *If* they set you off from here."

"Where else would they set me off from?"

"Some ways out in the Sargasso Sea, usually."

"Hmmm. Not auspicious.... Well, let's suppose I am given mercy. What would that entail?"

"Oh, well, then you get a full pint of water! *And* a frying pan you can try an' use as a paddle."

"In that case, I think I'd prefer to plead not guilty and take my chances."

"Well, it's your funeral."

With that as farewell, he made his exit.

The trial began promptly at three that same afternoon. While being led to the courtroom, I had my first glimpse of Nassau in daylight. I scanned the scene for usable data, trying to ascertain whether I'd entered the fictional world or not. Then I heard a telltale chugga-chugga. I turned to see an airship coming in from the sea—not as formidable-looking as the one which raided the S.S. *Paris*, but just as absurdly steam-powered.

Her Ladyship, or whatever her title was, took the bench to a chorus of cheers from the onlookers.

"Let's get on with it," she said. "I don't want this cutting into the cocktail hour."

The prosecutor, the fellow I had thought to be a pirate chief but evidently a rum-running associate of the judge, began by itemizing the losses the jurist had incurred in the unfortunate incident off Charleston. Halfway through it, my counsel at last voiced an objection.

"That's not right, Your Majesty," he told the court. "It wasn't twenty-seven cases of Scotch valued at seventeen hundred dollars. It was *seventeen* cases of Scotch valued at *twenty-seven* hundred dollars."

"I'll cede the point, Your Worshipfulness," the prosecutor replied gamely.

The gallery, at least, seemed highly amused. Bahamians appeared to be a jolly people, but I would have preferred their mirth not always come at my expense.

"Enough," the judge told them. "Is there any defense?"

"Well, against my advice, mind you, the defendant wishes to present testimony."

"Oh, Christ. All right. Get on with it."

As I took the stand I smiled at her—but I didn't make that mistake a second time. She looked now as if she'd just eaten an unripe apple.

"Your... Heavenly Magnificence," I opened. "I would like to begin by revealing a secret I felt not at liberty to disclose at our previous meeting."

"Then *do* it."

"Well, the truth is, I had a far more important mission than enforcing the, ah, quite repugnant ban on liquor sales."

"I don't see what's repugnant about Prohibition. I've done quite well by it."

The house roared—thank God I hadn't asked for a jury trial.

"And, no doubt, deservedly so," I groveled. "My true task involved something else entirely. I was sent out with one goal: to subdue the pirate menace! Most particularly, that branch of it which so recently made off with a bevy of young women from the S.S. *Paris*. One of whom was my own dear wife. Perhaps you are aware of the incident?"

"No, I am not. But what does it have to do with your theft?"

"These pirates arrived in a steam-powered airship...."

"So?"

"Well, where we come from, such craft are a novelty. There was some confusion as to how to bring them to justice, until finally I was given the airship which met its demise on the beach the other night. But the mission was to be kept a secret."

"Why?"

"Well, frankly, because few would believe it."

"I know *I* don't. This is gaining you nothing. Care to try another tack?"

"Yes, I would, if you don't mind. Might I assume yours is a world where deceit and cunning are priced at a premium?"

"In their proper place."

"Well, then, I'm your man. Deceit, cunning, and—when my survival's at risk—a keen sense of propriety. Describes me to a tee. Just allow me into your fold and I'll win back those paltry losses at Charleston before—"

I didn't have a chance to finish my address. The gavel fell with a sudden finality.

"Guilty. Sentence is the usual one. Time will be announced later."

"Do I at least get the frying pan?" I asked, but she'd already gone off for her gimlet or whatever it was she used to mark the end of a vexing day in court.

III

About eight that evening, the night jailer came up to the door of my cell.

"There's a visitor for ya. But you gots to talk through the hatch."

He went off and I peered into the darkened corridor to see a diminutive female silhouette.

"Is that you, Aggie?"

"Nah, it's the Duchess of Argyle come to invite you to tea. *Who the hell else would it be?*"

It was her, all right.

"I'm glad to see you. Listen, I think they're making plans for my coming-out party—disagreeable plans...."

"So?"

"Well, I've been thinking, there seems to be only the one guard at night, that feeble-looking old bimbo...."

"He's standing right here, you gink."

"Ah... marvelous."

"I heard you tried to hang the yarn about pirate-hunting on that kangaroo court this afternoon...."

"It's no yarn, Aggie. My wife was taken away by the fiends."

"What fiends?" the jailer asked.

"Pirates that came in a giant airship. They fell upon the steamship we were traveling on and abducted a gaggle of females."

"That right? I can think of only two men coulda pulled that off."

"Who?"

"The first is Jean Lafitte."

"Yeah? Wouldn't he be about 150 years old now?" Aggie asked.

"A descendant, must be. The second is... Jack Tigue."

"Jack Tigue? Say, isn't that the name of the boy in that book I was reading?" she asked me.

"Yes, one of Cousin Emmie's inventions."

"Who's Cousin Emmie?"

"The author of the book. She's also the one who came up with steam-powered airships."

"You seen 'em too?" she asked. "I couldn't figure out how they could work."

"Don't bother trying. I'm reluctant to confide this...."

"What?"

"The airship that attacked the S.S. *Paris* was steam-powered. I happened to consult Cousin Emmie about it, and she confirmed that just such a craft existed in her fictionalized world. Though according to her, it's not fictionalized at all."

"God damn. Your whole family is off its rocker."

"Well, I'd hate to have to argue the contrary. Nonetheless, I think you'll have a difficult time explaining steam-powered airships any other way. Or the existence of Jack Tigue."

"The name could just be a coincidence."

"Tell me, was this Jack Tigue ever involved with a circus?" I asked the jailer.

"So I've heard. They say that accounts for his success with the ladies."

"A contortionist?" Aggie asked him.

"Oh... I don't know if he goes in for that French stuff."

VIRTUE AT MARKET PRICE

"I don't suppose either he or this Lafitte have any women among their crew?" I asked.

"Not likely. They all fall in love with Jack, and he finds that a distraction. And Lafitte..."

"What about him?"

"Well, any he came across he'd probably find other uses for...."

"The heathen bastard!" Aggie's facade of cynical detachment showed a crack.

"He's that, all right. Brutal as all hell. Never gives quarter. But the women—"

He was cut short by a church bell ringing the half-hour.

"You better get out of here fast," he told Aggie. "The officer of the watch will be by any minute now."

"You'll come back, won't you?" I called after her. But she didn't reply.

For one long hour I sat alone with my thoughts—and they were none too pleasant. Now I had not only my own demise to consider, but Sesbania's possible descent into white slavery. Much as it pained me, I'd have to tap the nest egg I'd buried back at Andros Island.

When the old jailer passed on his rounds, I called him to the door.

"How would you like to share in a buried treasure?"

"What buried treasure?"

"Ten thousand dollars in gold. How does twenty percent strike you?"

"Not nearly so good as fifty percent. Where is it?"

"Andros Island. Just inland from where you'll find the remains of our airship. I have a little map here...."

He reached for it.

"No. We go together. Tomorrow night."

"Uh-uh. Once you're out the door, I got no way to keep you from runnin' off and leavin' me with nothin'. Then it's me they'd set adrift."

The old buzzard wasn't quite as thickheaded as I'd hoped. Still, it might be the last chance I'd have to bargain.

"All right." I held out my map. "X marks the spot. Distances in paces. That there is a sinkhole."

"The dingus?"

"Yes, the dingus. The gold weighs quite a bit. You won't have any trouble bringing it back to Nassau?"

"I'll handle it, don't you worry. And if it's there like you say, tomorrow midnight we can both make off.... By the way, that girl that was here... is she... taken?"

"Not that I'm aware. But be forewarned, she can be a little cantankerous."

"That's just how I like 'em!" He went off cackling.

The next day passed slowly, with only two interruptions to the torturous waiting. First, about ten, my so-called lawyer stopped by.

"Is there a chance of appeal?" I asked.

"You're not serious?"

"Then why are you here?"

"Oh. To let you know there's a ship leaving tomorrow at daybreak for the Azores. The captain's very kindly offered to take you along—partway, of course."

He enjoyed his little joke. I was coming to dislike Bahamians.

"Well, then, I'll start packing my trunk. Thanks for stopping by."

Just after lunch—beans and rice—Reverend Sweeting came by. He prayed for my soul and then handed me some religious tracts he took from a portfolio.

"Say, I don't suppose you have a copy of *Capt. Billy's Whiz Bang* in there?"

He did not. I spent the remainder of the afternoon reading about Job, the Old Testament's great masochist. I never quite understood the lesson one was supposed to take away from his story. Mindless obedience begot him nothing but misery. Why not earn it honestly by having a little fun?

At half past six, my co-conspirator finally arrived for his shift. Along with the dismal beans and rice, he brought me the distressing news that my booty had been purloined.

"You're kidding? No one knew about it but me."

"No, I ain't kiddin'. All that was there was a hole. An' this book." He held up the rhyming dictionary. "I thought I might keep it for my trouble."

"Be my guest. Maybe you can compose a ballad in my honor. I'm told I set sail at first light."

"I'll see what I can come up with. Well, you know what they say: money's round so's it can run away...."

I found his cavalier attitude irksome. Nonetheless, I did have reason to believe his story. If he'd uncovered ten thousand in gold, would he show up that evening for his shift at a dingy jail? Or be so polite as to ask permission to keep the rhyming dictionary?

Even so, I couldn't bring myself to tell him about the second stash. I'd allowed far too much treasure to slip through my hands during the recent past to risk that.

There was nothing for it now but hope I could come up with a plan to win over the accommodating captain I'd be meeting on the morrow. In the meantime, I reread some of the more vivid passages of Job's story. It's amazing how easily a disheartened soul can find cheer in the suffering of others.

I'd been dozing—half-asleep, half-awake—when I heard a distinctive "Pssst" at my door.

"It's me, Aggie. Come on."

She was trying to unlock the door.

"You got the keys from him! Did you knock him out?"

"No...." She tried another key. "If you really want to know, I made a deal...." She turned away as her words trailed off.

"Oh... Well. I'm sincerely touched you'd go to such lengths.... And I don't think anyone would think less of you.... I hope it wasn't too—"

"What *the hell* are you mumbling about?" She finally found the right key and opened the door. "Did you think *I*... With *him?* For *you?* Jesus Christ, if you aren't the most arrogant son-of-a-bitch...."

"Then how?"

"That loot you buried."

"Oh. So it was you? I would have thought such a thing as thievery beneath a journalist of your repute, Miss Ready."

"Well, ain't you somethin'? I save ya from a sure death, and all you can do is bellyache about how I did it!"

"Sorry. I'd just been counting on that loot...."

"What good would it do ya out there swimmin' with the fishes?"

"I was expecting a last-minute reprieve."

"Well, that's just what you got. But you give me any more of your grousing and it will be bon voyage, mucker! You got it?"

"Yes, all right."

She led me down the corridor, past the empty guard station, to a door that opened on an alley.

"Now, here's the deal I made with the head jane: I sneak you out of here, then we leave town P.D.Q. and never come back. She don't want no one else to know she's been bought off with trinkets."

"You found the jewels?"

"Didn't I just say so?"

"You said loot. I assumed you meant the gold coins."

"Yeah, I got those too."

"Good. And for your trouble, I'll gladly give you, say... two thousand?"

"Jesus, don't you take the cake? Well, forget it. There ain't nothin' left to give no one."

"Where'd that go?"

"Financing our getaway, sap."

"Ten thousand dollars? How are we traveling, private yacht?"

"You'll see."

We slunk from alley to alley until we came to the area of the harbor.

"Here she is," Aggie announced, nodding toward an airship.

Unlike Wilbur, she was a true dirigible, and thus, ironically, rigid. She looked a little long in the tooth, with steam periodically venting from outtakes far above us. But at least she seemed airworthy.

"We're going to need a crew."

"Oh, I took care of that too. Come on."

As you might well imagine, I was more than a little dispirited on entering the ship to find the crew virtually identical with the one that had so recently betrayed me to the rum-runners. At least they had the decency to avert their gazes.

"There is one other minor obstacle," I noted. "None of us knows how to fly a craft of this sort."

"Yeah, so I figured. That's why I hired a couple cracks." She went over to one of several doors which led off the control room and knocked. A black man emerged, buttoning his shirt. "Meet Horatio. He knows all there is about working one of these things. Or so he tells me."

"Oh, yes," he said. "There ain't nothin' I don't know about workin' on an airship, or Lucy in particular."

He was West Indian, but didn't speak with the same accent as the Bahamians. By then a woman had followed him out. Lucy, I assumed, until Aggie introduced her as Mattie.

"And what's Mattie's expertise?" I asked.

"Keepin' Horatio's buttons on."

CHAPTER 7.

DINNER FOR TWO, OR, THE OFFAL TRUTH

"We need to set course for Tortuga," Aggie announced.

"Which Tortuga?"

"What do you mean, which Tortuga?"

"Well, there's the Dry Tortugas...."

"Then it ain't that one. This one will be plenty wet—
they say it's a pirate haven."

"That would be the island off Haiti, famous in
swashbuckler lore. How fast can this thing go, Horatio?"

"Well, that all depends."

"Depends on what?"

"Is it day, or night; is the sun shining, or is it
cloudy."

"Are you saying we need sunlight to make steam?"

"Sure. A good head of steam. Otherwise, it's *man the
oars!*"

"Man the oars?"

He led me up a ladder to a large open room. There,
lining either side, were two banks of four oars.

"Do you mean to tell me the ship can be propelled
simply by rowing the air?"

"Hah! That's crazy! Row the sky?"

"Then what?"

"Oh—well, the rowin' boils the water... somehow or
other. All very mysterious. And that's what makes the
steam."

This was my first and last attempt at understanding
how a steam-powered airship functioned. Not surprising-

ly, Cousin Emmie hadn't bothered to work out the details. How manning the oars could possibly bring water
to a boil would have to remain a dark secret. As for
Horatio, his facility in running the ship seemed to de-
pend not so much on any expertise as on a deep-seated
faith.

We left our mooring and had just enough residual
steam to head out over the harbor. But since it was still
some hours before sunrise, I ordered eight men to go up
and man the oars. They grumbled, of course. But if I'd
learned one thing during the ill-fated cruise aboard
Wilbur, it was never coddle a crew. I picked out the
scrawniest of the malingerers and held a cutlass to his
throat.

"Open the hatch, Mr. Cartwright."

The CPO hesitated. But when none of the others
seemed inclined to interfere, he complied. I could see the
reflection of the moon in the water below.

"All right, Brubecker, what do you have to say for
yourself now?" I asked.

"I ain't Brubecker...."

His protestation annoyed me, causing me to act impulsively. There was a splash below.

"Let that be a lesson to all of you: never correct me
before other members of the crew."

I believe my newfound mettle surprised the men,
but none more than me. Well, except maybe the fellow
not named Brubecker. We weren't more than forty feet
above the water, so there was no reason to think he
hadn't survived the fall. After that, unfortunately, the
odds ran against him. One of the great ironies of the
Navy is that not one in ten ordinary seamen knows how
to swim.

"Close the hatch, Mr. Cartwright."

Before he could do so, a parrot flew up through the opening.

"*Ahoy there, skeezicks!*"

It was the same damned parrot.

"An extra ration of rum to the man who kills the bird."

"Hey! Leave 'im alone!" Aggie counter-ordered. It flew to her shoulder and cackled. No doubt their shared antipathy for me had caused them to bond.

The chosen seven—plus one replacement—trudged up to man the oars.

"Set course on heading 120 degrees, due southeast, Horatio. Quick as she'll go."

"Aye, aye, sir."

"By the way, what's the name of the ship?"

"*Lucy's Revenge,*" he told me.

"Who's Lucy?"

"A working girl, in Port Royal."

"Ah…. Miss Ready, I wonder if I could have a word in my cabin."

"Not on your life—*lug.*"

Apparently, Horatio's use of the term "working girl" immediately preceding my request had led her to a misapprehension.

"You flatter yourself, my dear. I merely wish a consultation. And don't bring that damned bird."

"*He's got himself a cabin boy!*" it squawked.

"Watch it!" Aggie snarled at the bird.

The parrot flew over to Horatio's shoulder and she followed me into my cabin.

"I thank you for negotiating my release, Aggie. But I can't say I'm altogether pleased you paid ten thousand dollars in gold for an imaginary ship named for a venereal disease."

"Oh, give it air! I wasn't the one who let the cat out of the bag. Somehow that Littko dame knew exactly how much gold you had. Now, how d'ya account for that?"

"Ah... I might have mentioned the figure in negotiating with that jailer."

"Big-mouth."

"But I never mentioned the jewels."

"Well, I paid her the jewels in exchange for lettin' you out."

"How'd you know where they were?"

"I watched ya buryin' 'em, ya gink. The ladies' lounge wasn't fifty yards away. I went back the next day and dug up all the books, then hired a boat to get 'em to Nassau. I heard the Littko dame was the one in charge, so I offered her some jewels for lettin' you out. She ended up takin' 'em all. Then when I asked about buying one of her airships—she seems to have a monopoly on the things—she named a price of ten thousand in gold. I got her down to nine, so I'd have enough to get supplies, and hire Horatio. And that's how we ended up with a ship christened with the clap. Anyway, can you think of a better name for a booze-runner full of blistering jack-shites?"

"Point taken. Speaking of which, how'd you convince the crew to sign on?"

"They needed to eat. Everything runs pretty dear in a place like that. And none of the rum-runners would trust them."

"Wise men."

"And *woman*."

"But what makes you sure *we* can trust them?"

"Well, for one thing, they ain't got guns."

"No guns?"

"Haven't you noticed? There aren't any guns in this... whatever it is."

She was right. In fact, I hadn't seen even a pistol since our crash.

"What exactly changed your mind about me, and my story?" I asked.

"Too many things I couldn't explain. Like, why's nobody got any guns. And how come there ain't no cars, or trucks, *at all?*"

"Well, maybe the place is just a little backward."

"Uh-uh. I asked—they had no idea what the hell I was talking about. Didn't know about airplanes, either."

"Strange."

"Yeah, *too* strange. So I got to thinkin' maybe there was something to your story."

"I see. But tell me, why didn't you just keep the gold and jewels for yourself?"

"I want to meet this Jack Tigue. And I figured I'd need help finding him—*and* gettin' back home again."

"You realize he's probably just a figment of Cousin Emmie's imagination."

"So you say. But either way, just think of the story I'm going to get out of this.... Hell, I'll nab a Pulitzer, for sure. By the way, how *do* we get back?"

"Your guess is as good as mine."

"Yer kiddin'?"

"I wish I was. Maybe heading into a storm... or else out of one."

"Ah, don't be screwy.... But tell me, what else does your cousin have to say about this Jack Tigue? He was still a kid in the tale I read."

"Well, there are subsequent books that mention him. The most bizarre she calls *The Circensiad.* It's a sort of blending of equal parts *Toby Tyler,* Emmie's psychotic musings, and a book by a guy named Virgil, called *The Aeneid.* Maybe you've heard of it?"

"Of course I've heard of it, you gink! Didn't I go to Barnard?"

"You went to Barnard? The little sister to Columbia?"

"Call it that again and I'll carve you a second keister! Get me? And don't look so incredulous. Can't a dame crack wise once in a while without growin' up in a tenement?"

This girl grew stranger by the minute. Worse, I was beginning to find her almost irresistibly attractive. Her shirt had become unbuttoned during her excited defense of her alma mater and I reached over to button it. The back of my hand brushed across a nipple which seemed to be at full alert. Her lips twitched.... There'd be no stopping things now....

Or, at least, one might be forgiven for having thought so. Not her, however. It was precisely at that moment her pointy-toed shoe connected with my shin.

"I seen that look in your eyes! You got a wife to save—remember, mug? Let's keep this to business, just so no one gets hurt."

"All right." I casually stepped back, out of kicking distance. "What makes you believe Jack Tigue is in Tortuga?"

"From what I hear, he stops by there real regular. To see a woman. But we're going to have to play it careful with him."

"I'm good at that—playing it careful. What about Lafitte?"

"They say he hangs out on the Gulf Coast. Has a place in the bayous somewhere." She yawned. "Now I need some sleep. Ain't had more than an hour since you crashed Wilbur. Better not be so careless with *Lucy*— we're out of gold."

"I'll keep that in mind. Oh, be sure to lock your door."

"No need. I'll be sleeping with this under my pillow." She held up a folding straight razor. "So if you need me, make sure you knock...."

She left and I now had a chance to assess the accommodations. The cabin itself was a good deal larger than the one I'd had on Wilbur. One of the advantages of traveling on a vessel of Cousin Emmie's invention was that interior dimensions weren't governed by external ones. And it came with certain amenities, most felicitous among them a decanter of brandy. I took a long swig. Then I sat down at the desk and recorded my first entry in the ship's log:

Wife missing. Money gone. Crew unreliable. First mate unapproachable. Ship a phantasm. Expect death imminent.

Succinct, but I wasn't sure I liked the ending. I took another long draught and tried looking at things more philosophically. Perhaps they weren't as bad as they seemed.

For instance, maybe we'd catch up with Tigue on a day he wasn't feeling his best. After all, pirates are well known to revel to excess. And wasn't I better off without the distraction of promised reward and buried treasure? At least now I could focus all my attention on recovering my beloved (supposed) wife. And hopefully before her virtue had been compromised. If the fiends took that from her, chances were slim they'd miss the fifteen thousand strapped immediately to its north.

On my next trip back to the decanter, I noticed an odd print hanging above the desk: some sort of sea creature having its way with a mermaid. Or at least attempting to.... Just how do mermaids reproduce, anyway? I picked it up to get a closer look, but the artist—apparently an impressionist—had left it to the viewer's imagination to solve the conundrum; the anatomy was kept vague. Unlike that which I now espied through the peephole that had been hidden behind the print. Aggie was undressing....

Once more she looked the innocent maiden, still unsullied (that is, from what I could see) by life's cruelties. Surveying the ivory slope leading from her smooth, arched back to her modest, yet pert, fanny, I found it easy to forget she'd only minutes before brandished a straight razor in a way that could only be termed chilling.

When she got into bed, I replaced the print and sat down for a long tête-à-tête with the decanter. Eventually, my thoughts returned to my primary female and her predicament. I considered changing course for the Gulf. From what I'd heard in Nassau, Lafitte was the more likely pirate to have absconded with the women. And he would also pose the greater threat to Sesbania's well-being.

Then again, he would also pose the greater threat to *my* well-being. So Tortuga it was. We made about thirty-five knots under oar power, and sixty after the sun rose above the thin clouds. With any luck we'd reach the island by noon.

Just after morning mess, I assembled the men, striking the sternest mien I could muster.

"First things first: those articles agreed to aboard Wilbur died with him. There won't be any more vote taking. Objections? Good. We're flying at 800 feet currently and the waters below are reputed to be shark-infested.... Our primary mission remains to seek out those pirates who stripped the S.S. *Paris* of her precious cargo.... But rest assured, I bear no affection for rum-runners. Especially after my treatment while their guest in Nassau. When time and circumstances allow, we will prey on them with a merciless fury!"

Cheers all around. Except for Horatio.

"Can't say I'd recommend that tack. It sounds like we'll be battling pretty near everyone."

"The U.S. Navy will be on our side. And the Coast Guard."

"They don't seem to be itching for a fight themselves. Don't make too many appearances outside the twelve-mile limit. And can't even manage to evict Lafitte and his gang from Louisiana."

He'd unfortunately set the crew to thinking, a hazard considered by naval officers equal to icebergs and U-boats. I suggested he go to his quarters for some rest. He agreed, then requested Mattie join him to sew on some buttons. From the sounds emerging a little later, I took it she was a high-spirited seamstress.

Their confab seemed likely to set the men on new lines of thought, and I became anxious for the safety of my first mate. In order to divert their attention once more, I issued them their rum ration. With benefit of hindsight, one could call it a slight error in judgment.

It was the damn parrot that started things. He led them in a rousing rendition of *Ballochy Bill the Sailor*—the seaman's anthem. With only one fair young maiden available, they prepared to lay siege to the door of Aggie's cabin.

I stepped between them and it. "Stand down, all of you!"

"Or?"

I was saved having to answer when Aggie herself opened the door and slid past me. Rather than acting cowed, she seemed eager to cavort. Albertson, nearly twice her size, joined her and they began dancing to the song's chorus. He pulled her into an embrace. I moved to separate them, but before I could, she shook him. A half second later, her right arm swung quickly across his left one. He gave out a frightful cry, then held up his hand. Blood was flowing where his pinky had but recently resided.

A thoroughly amused Aggie picked up her trophy, wiped her razor on the sleeve of her white blouse, and again took up the dance, offering herself as partner to the others of the crew. This time, there were no takers.

II

Due to some minor errors in navigation, it wasn't until well after midnight that we sighted Tortuga. I think it deserves to be noted, however, these errors could only partly be attributed to myself. The charts on board were worse than rudimentary. What's more, the geography was often simply wrong. I believe Cousin Emmie bears the blame for that. Traditionally, Tortuga has sat to the north of Haiti. In her confused world, it lay to the south. Nevertheless, we did find it eventually.

We could see the lights of a town below, but I purposely circled around to a more secluded area just beyond.

"Horatio and I will descend and reconnoiter... and you, Albertson." As we were to masquerade as buccaneers, I figured the bloody hand would lend us authenticity.

"I'm comin' too," Aggie insisted.

"I don't think that would be a good idea. The men down there are likely to be ruthless and unspeakably cruel."

"Ah, ishkabibble. Ain't I worked the theatrical beat? You don't know from cruel and ruthless, mister. Not 'til ya meet them prima donnas."

With no time to argue, I conceded. In truth, she may have looked the most pirate-like of any of us. Notably flat-chested, she'd already been dressing like a man. And the severed finger she now wore from a thin gold chain about her neck did much to deflect notice from her more feminine features.

As did the loud-mouthed parrot perched on her shoulder and echoing her every line: "*Ah, ishkabibble. Ain't I worked the theatrical beat? You don't know from cruel and ruthless, mister.*"

I wasn't altogether sanguine about leaving Cartwright in charge, but the crew had been taking turns at the oars for the past several hours and appeared too exhausted to get into mischief. Just the same, I double-checked that both Mattie and the rum were secure under lock and key.

We repelled down to the rocky island and made our way gingerly. The moon was out, but the footing uncertain. We finally entered the town proper about three. It seemed to consist solely of barrooms, bordellos, tattoo parlors, and armorers, with most combining at least three of the four trades.

For pirates, of course, three a.m. is the height of the evening. The crowds were lively, and not wanting to appear conspicuous, we entered the liveliest of all the establishments: *Le Pélican Débauché*. For the sake of the non-francophone, the proprietor had added an illustration which left little doubt as to his intention. Yes, some pirate was doing unto the poor bird just what my nemesis Gilbert had appeared to be doing to that goat.

Inside, men and women of all races—and a fascinating variety of inclinations—were carousing with a gusto and athleticism that would shame your typical waterfront riffraff, what with their relatively timid viewpoints on depravity. There was a good deal of song, and some very strident discourse. But in such a babel of languages that little of it was understandable. Something like what one encounters any evening on Coney Island.

I soon lost track of Albertson. But every once in a while I would hear him lending his voice to some bawdy sea chantey. He was particularly good with the repetitious choruses, which more often than not consisted of a catalogue of crude euphemisms for ladies' parts and accessories.

"There's a fellow I sailed under a few years back," Horatio told me. "Maybe, I should see what I can find out."

"Yes, see if he has any information about the abduction of young women from the S.S. *Paris*. Or on the whereabouts of this Jack Tigue."

I turned around just in time to see Aggie dragged onto the dance floor. The outfit, flat chest, bloodied sleeve, and severed finger dangling from her neck may have obscured her gender, but not her softer features. She looked like a young boy—a sadistic one, to be sure—

but a boy nonetheless. And for a pirate of a certain bent...
Well, sadism is all part of the fun.

I imagined right about then she regretted her rash
decision to come into town with us, and I was mere
seconds from coming to her aid when a large hand fell
upon my shoulder.

"Madame would like to see you."

The hand belonged to a black man who spoke with a
French accent and wore the livery of an eighteenth-
century footman.

I looked over at Aggie. She had her razor out and
was taking swipes at her dance partner. Risky, perhaps,
but the crowd seemed with her.

The footman led me up the broad stairs in the center
of the room and across a wide mezzanine. He opened a
door and stepped aside. I went in, and he shut the door.

It was a huge room, lavishly furnished—and vict-
ualed—but seemingly uninhabited. Then I heard a telltale
whoosh, and a woman appeared at what had been a
hidden door.

"I needed to make myself ready for you." She
laughed at her remark, then lifted her elaborate skirts
and sashayed over to a large couch. "Come here and sit
beside me."

She was a strikingly beautiful black woman—tall,
high-cheekboned and -bosomed, with full lubricious lips,
and costumed as one of Marie Antoinette's ladies-in-
waiting. She didn't need to issue a second invitation. I sat
down in the middle of the couch, and she leaned in
toward me, running her hand through my hair.

"Yes... When I heard you were here, my mouth wa-
tered! You are one of the few I see who knows to look
after his toilette. I like the baby mustache. These pi-

rates... with their foul smells, and bloody sores... They make me ill! You wouldn't believe...."

She went on at some length about the negative consequences for a lady of breeding who takes a pirate lover. However, in doing so, she revealed so thorough a knowledge of the subject there could be little chance it had been acquired secondhand. What made the encounter particularly uncanny was that she seemed very certain she knew me. In fact, she claimed to have seen me only a week before. On this, I felt sure she was mistaken. I very definitely would have remembered her.

By now her mouth was on mine and the authenticity of her French inflection quickly confirmed by her remarkably agile tongue. Retracting it, she turned and leaned back onto me. Then she tugged a little ribbon and her bodice fell swiftly open. She led my hands toward her heaving twins, but I had a pretty good idea what she had in mind and took over operations.

Her reaction seemed decidedly positive, yet after some minutes she grew restless and drew one of my hands down her belly. I soon found what she'd sent me after and proceeded to give the little man in the boat a ride he'd not soon forget.

My hostess seemed pleased. She indicated this firstly by kicking a tray of aperitifs from the table beside the couch to the far end of the room, and secondly by reaching back her arms and trying to pull my head to her abdomen. Her arms were surprisingly strong, and rather than have my head detached, I spun around on top of her. From there, she pushed me down on the floor. We both seemed to be thinking along the same lines.

By then, the problematic skirts had disappeared and I found myself planted between two of the most shapely thighs I'd ever set eyes on—and this from a man who's spent a good deal of time in the close company of thighs. In spite of—or maybe due to—the whacking I'd given him earlier, the little man in the boat stood tall. But now he was in for some truly rough weather. The licking I gave him rivaled that of the seas lashing Cape Horn. Yet, through it all, he remained at his post.

The lady in hand did not recite Latin, nor make any particularly distinctive noise at all. Her manner of expression was far more demonstrative. A console sat just behind the couch, covered with a menagerie of glass bibelots. One by one, these made their way to the wall opposite.

When the last of the animal kingdom lay shattered, she pulled me to the dining table. Bottles of wine, decanters of liqueurs, and plates of delicacies lined two sides. But the center and other two sides were barren. She pulled down my pants and laid herself down on the table, knees spread high and pelvis thrust nearly to the edge of the table. She was a commendably accommodating young lady.

Well, I suppose you can guess what happened next. Plates, bottles, glassware—but only, I'm afraid, through the first and second courses. Though I did my best to fulfill my obligations as honored guest, the preliminaries had brought me to a high level of excitement. To be honest, I'd never set any records at this stage of the game. Which is one reason why I put so much effort into wearing down my opponent in the earlier rounds.

The lady lying before me, however, had *not* been worn down. In fact, she wasn't even winded.

"What sort of man are you?"

"Well, one does one's best...."

She sent a bottle in the direction of my head—claret, I think, but perhaps a burgundy.

"Clarisse!" someone called from outside the open window. "You alone?"

"Yes, Jack. Yes. Just give me a moment...." In two shakes of a brass monkey's tail, she'd hopped off the table and reassembled her costume. "Get!" she told me in a very persuasive whisper.

III

I was still pulling up my trousers when she slammed the door closed—much to the amusement of those frolicking on the mezzanine. You've never seen so many toothless grins. By the time I'd buttoned up, Clarisse had recommenced serving dinner back in her room. Wine first, several bottles in quick succession exploding on the other side of the wall. Then the entrée; I believe it must have been turkey—nothing less could have produced so weighty a thud, or brought down such a quantity of plaster. More toothless grins.

You'd think a pirate port would be the perfect place for a dentist to hang his shingle. Then again, any service involving pain and a client armed with a cutlass must count as a risky business.

Horatio bounded up the stairs and pushed his way toward me.

"There's a rumor Jack Tigue is here on the island."

"Is he? Then I believe he may be finishing my meal in there." I nodded toward the door just as a large piece of glassware splintered on the far side. "It might be best to let him eat in peace."

"And then what?"

"Good question. What do you know about him? Is he approachable?"

"Well, like most pirates, he's mainly after the loot."

"What about the torturing of prisoners and that sort of thing?"

"No, he has little time for torturing. What with all his women..."

"Well, I suggest we leave him alone until he's slept off the meal. Between the four of us, we should be able to subdue him. Though his lady friend could prove a problem."

"Clarisse? Yes, she's a handful, all right."

"So you know her?"

"I used to be her footman. Worked my way up from there—if you understand me."

"Yes, I think I do. Ever make it to dessert?"

"Oh, yes. And sometimes a late supper. Unfortunately, she became angry with me."

"Yes, she is rather demanding."

"Demanding?" He shrugged. "No, my mistake was to ask for a raise. She called me a Bolshevik and had me tossed out."

"Then weren't you afraid to show your face here?"

"Well, that was some years ago. I doubt she remembers me. I doubt she remembers anyone...."

"Except Jack Tigue?"

"Yes, except Jack."

"What's he got that women find so irresistible?"

"Who knows? I've heard rumors... but too fantastic to be believed...."

"You must tell me sometime. But first we should find the others. Is Aggie still performing downstairs?"

"No—I have some bad news about her."

"They realized she was a woman?"

"Well, not 'til later. A fellow comes up, to dance with her, but he seems to want her finger."

"The bloody stub she wore around her neck?"

"Yes. He keeps reaching for it.... She gets angry, takes her razor and says, 'Here! Have one of your own.'"

"Oh.... And I suppose he objected?"

"He did, but too late. And you know something strange about that guy?"

"Frankly, strange is all I've known for the last six weeks. But I'll bite. What was strange about the guy?"

"He looked just like your man Albertson. Like his twin brother."

"You sure it wasn't Albertson wanting back his finger?"

"No, he had all his fingers—before she sliced one off for him. Only his was from the other hand."

"So now a mirror image of Albertson."

"Yes. Anyway, it turns out this twin is Lafitte's first mate, Geoff l'Indigné."

"He's called Indignant Jeff?"

"By his friends."

"Is Lafitte here?"

"Was here. He thought Aggie's trick very funny."

"That was lucky."

"Well, not so lucky. He thought it funny, but said she'd still get a flogging. He thought that funny, too. They take her outside and tear off her shirt...."

"And spilled the beans, so to speak...."

"Yes. The beans were right out in the open."

"And he flogged her anyway?"

"No, he seemed to take a liking to her. Had her bundled up in a rug and carried off to his ship."

"Damn! If only I'd been there to stop it!"

"Yes, me too."

"Where were you?"

"Hiding in the back of the crowd. I guess now you want to go after Lafitte?"

"Well, I'm afraid the code requires it."

"Which code? Not the pirate code. On women, the pirate code says: easy come, easy go."

"I was speaking of the chivalric code."

"Well, it's not like she was much of a lady...."

"Perhaps not. But she did save me from being marooned at sea."

"Yes, but only by giving up your own money."

"You aren't doing much for my resolve, Horatio. We've got to at least make an attempt at getting her back, or we'd never be able to live with ourselves."

"Oh, I think I could."

"Nonsense, all men to their duty! Now let's find Albertson and get back to the ship."

"He's lying in the gutter just outside. I don't think he's used to drinking like a pirate."

In an effort to mitigate his stench, we gave Albertson a dunking in a rain barrel. Unfortunately, it only made things worse. And for good reason. No sooner had we pulled him out than a girl leaned out of a window and poured a chamber pot into the receptacle. Horatio tied a rope to the reeking gob and we pulled him along to where *Lucy* was waiting.

On boarding, we found a line of men with loose buttons waiting to petition Mattie. She'd opened her door to them and handled them all good-naturedly—sewing on their buttons but nothing more. Mattie seemed to treat everything good-naturedly. She was a native Bahamian and it took some time before I could consistently make out her words. When I later inquired of Horatio if they were married, he just laughed.

"Did Lafitte drop any hints where he was going?" I asked him now.

"Said they sail at dawn, for 'you know where.'"

"No, I don't know."

"Neither do I. But I suppose his men did."

"Well, let's assume Louisiana. He'll have a two-hour head start on us...."

"How do you figure?"

"I thought you said they were to sail at dawn?"

"*Pirate dawn.* That would be about noon regular."

"Excellent. Then we can get ahead of him and wait in ambush. Can we make our own cloud?"

"Yes, but it's better to find a real one. A steam cloud is all hot and sticky."

"All right, we'll look for a real one."

"You sure you want to tangle with Lafitte? I know a friendly bar in Havana. Pretty girls. Why not go there instead?"

"Make way, dammit! All ahead two-thirds!"

"Two-thirds? Two-thirds of what?"

"Two-thirds of whatever full speed is given current conditions."

"Is this an arithmetic problem?"

"No, it's not a damn arithmetic problem!"

"Well, the sun is out. We should be able to go pretty fast."

"All right. All ahead something less than pretty fast."

I set course for the northwest and the Straits of Florida. Lafitte would probably be hunting rum-runners on his way to Louisiana, and the passage between Cuba and

Florida was likely to be flush with them—assuming, that is, Cuba and Florida were in their customary proximity to one another. There was every possibility Cousin Emmie had placed one or the other among the Spice Islands....

A foul smell permeated the cabin, and it wasn't long before I pinpointed it.

"Have we a crow's nest?" I asked Horatio.

"Oh, yes. Straight up the ladder from the oar deck."

I retrieved a bottle of rum from the locker and handed it to Albertson.

"You'd better go up there and keep watch," I told him, then turned back to Horatio. "What do we have in the way of armament?"

"Armament?"

"Well, traditionally, pirate ships came equipped with cannons. Very useful things in ship-to-ship combat."

"Oh, we have cannons."

"Really? But no firearms? Where are they?"

"The gun deck, of course. Come."

He led me into the galley. There he took a chicken from a cage, then climbed a ladder to a section of the ship behind the oar deck. It contained large boilers, and a mishmash of steam pipes running in every direction. It was hot, but not quite so hot as you might imagine. Perhaps because there were no apparent sources of heat beneath the boilers. Stranger still, there were no crewmen manning the place. Most of the pipes went out to the large steam engines along the sides. There were six of them altogether, each with a pair of pistons powering a shaft which led to a propeller at least ten feet in diameter.

We climbed up a steel ladder on the port side and reached a long, narrow gallery running the length of the ship. There was, he told me, another like gallery on the starboard side. Steam pipes came up from below and fed into pressure tanks. A second set of pipes led off the tanks horizontally and ended about a foot short of the outer wall of the ship. These horizontal pipes—apparently the guns' barrels—were about five inches in diameter and hinged at roughly half their length. Horatio opened one by lifting the outside end into a vertical position, then pointed to the bore of the stationary end.

"You see, you put your ammunition here." He pushed the chicken in, a scrawny fryer, then closed the barrel by restoring the outer half to its horizontal position. "Now, we open the gun port...." He flipped open a hatch beyond the barrel. A gust of air rushed in. "Then..."

He pulled a lever at the base of the barrel and there was a loud report. I'd always assumed domestic fowl had lost the ability to fly, but apparently not entirely. The blast seemed to provoke some primal instinct in the bird. It shot straight out over the ocean about two hundred yards, but from there traveled under its own power. Last seen, it was making its way for the Cuban coast.

"I suppose that should work. But what do we use for ammunition? Surely not our food supply?"

He pointed to some wooden barrels lining the back wall. As I approached one, I noted an off-putting odor. Far more off-putting than even Albertson's.

My next memory was of Horatio holding me up to the open gun port.

"You OK? Shouldn't go near the ammunition without a gas mask."

"What in God's name is in those barrels?"

"Offal. Grade A-one."

"Are you saying we shoot rotting animal guts at each other?"

"Yes—if we can get them. Sometimes we must settle for manure, things like that."

"And the range?"

"Offal, three hundred yards. Manure, not so far."

After an extended sojourn with the brandy decanter in my cabin, I returned to the control room and queried Horatio about Lafitte's ship.

"Oh, in general outline, not so different from our *Lucy*."

"How's it differ?"

"It's big. Very big. With many guns. And the crew..."

"What about the crew? Is it much larger than ours?"

"Larger, and meaner... And full of lust—comes from eatin' so many prawns, Mattie says."

I went back to my cabin and the brandy decanter.

CHAPTER 8.

EVERY PIRATE HIS HAREM

Lucy had been a rum-running jade, and she sported a chemise of camouflage suitable to that profession: on her underside, a light sky-blue with wisps of white cloud breaking up her contours, and above, an even coat of sea-green. The idea being to make detection difficult for both Coast Guard vessels patrolling below and pirate airships flying above.

It was these latter that posed the far greater danger, Horatio explained. *Lucy* was armed, but solely for defensive purposes. If it came to a battle with a pirate ship, he told me, she would almost certainly lose.

"Her only hope," he concluded, "is to outrun the pirate.... Why not head for that bar in Havana I was tellin' you about?"

"No. We may not be as well armed, but we can still outwit him."

"Outwit him how?"

"Like I said before, ambush him. We'll hide in a cloud and let him pass. Then cross his stern and fire on his rudder. If we can disable that, he'll be dead in the water, so to speak."

"Not a bad plan, I guess."

"What do you mean, you guess? You don't think blasting offal at it will foul his rudder?"

"Well, depends how you mean foul."

"Disable, render useless."

"Maybe, maybe not. But it *will* make it smell very, very bad."

As we headed into the Straits, a providential bank of clouds rolled in from the north. I took the ship up to three thousand feet, then cut back the engines to just enough to maintain position.

"Will Lafitte travel above or below the clouds?" I asked Horatio.

"Depends. If he's hunting the rum-runners on the sea, below. He'd run slower, but still faster than a ship. If he's hunting airships, he'll fly above the clouds."

"Let's assume he'll stay above since he's heading for home and will want to make time. That is, if he doesn't mind the cold."

"Cold?"

"It can get pretty brisk at six thousand feet."

"Oh, not when you got steam heat."

There was also no need to worry about pressure height, or the myriad other bothersome principles of airship physics Emmie was unacquainted with. There's no denying, the fictional life comes with some real advantages. Unless, I imagine, you find yourself in a Russian novel, or something by Zola. Then all bets are off.

I took *Lucy* to fifty-five hundred feet, near the top of our cloud cover. There we waited. To lessen the crew's nervous tension, I had the rum ration issued. Then the next day's. And when that didn't do the trick, those for the following week.

Their mood now might best be described as buoyant. Too buoyant, in fact. Horatio took the precaution of locking Mattie in their cabin with a pair of cutlasses.

About an hour later, a garbled message came down the voice tube from the crow's nest. Pretty much any communication emanating from Albertson that didn't involve a closed fist came garbled. But this one notably so. The only thing we could all agree on was that it had begun with the words "Holy Christ!"

I assumed he'd been facing forward and Lafitte's gigantic ship had startled him while passing overhead.

"Take a crew and man the guns, Horatio."

He picked three men and handed out gas masks. "But who will man the shovel? I don't think these will be enough...."

"Someone fetch Albertson. It can't smell much worse than he does himself, and he'll have consumed that bottle by now. I'll try to approach on the port side. And remember, aim for the rudder. Take us to six thousand feet, Mr. Cartwright. And alert the forward lookouts."

We rose quickly. When there were no sightings, I took us up another five hundred feet.

Within seconds, the starboard lookout reported: "Airship ten degrees to starboard—and a damned big one!"

"What's its speed?" I asked.

"About forty knots."

We were in the sun now. I took us to full speed, banked to port, then swung hard to starboard. We could see it now and were approaching just as I'd hoped, crossing its stern barely a hundred yards away.

"Fire when ready!" I yelled into the tube to the gun deck.

We were slightly above Lafitte's ship and I had an unobstructed view of the barrage. One after another the air cannons fired their pestilent sludge. There was no way to ascertain what damage we'd caused to his rudder, but we'd certainly rendered it a good deal less attractive.

When we had passed, I did a wide turn about and we raked them with the starboard battery. The pirate's vessel slowed, then seemed to come adrift in the wind.

"Ha! Just as I expected. He's immobilized."

A minute later, the enemy ship was engulfed in a cloud of steam.

"That won't do him any good," I said, a little prematurely.

We cheered as Horatio returned with the gun crew—if only briefly. You read about offal, but until you've spent some time in its company, it's difficult to imagine its lingering effects.

By now the steam had cleared from where Lafitte's craft had last been sighted. It was nowhere to be seen. We scanned the skies.

Then, quite suddenly, the pirate appeared off our starboard bow, running at seventy knots and looking distressingly immaculate.

"He's steam-cleaned himself!" Cartwright announced.

"No use, looks like," Horatio added. "I think we only made him angry."

It seemed wise to keep our bow toward Lafitte's ship, so he couldn't get a clear shot at our own rudder. "Take us to fifteen thousand feet, Mr. Cartwright. By the way, Horatio, what's our maximum altitude?"

"Not sure, but let's hope it's more than fifteen thousand."

When we passed twelve thousand, *Lucy* began emitting noises. At first, they were vague groans. But five hundred feet further on, she assumed the spirit of a banshee. The screeching was unbearable. Then a pipe burst and filled the control room with steam.

"Maximum altitude about twelve thousand feet, Captain," Horatio informed me.

"Yes, thank you. Let's take it all the way down to five hundred feet, Mr. Cartwright. I doubt he'll be expecting that."

Unfortunately, he *was* expecting that. No sooner had we passed through the floor of the cloud bank than he was on our stern. We heard the bangs of his air cannons, then a series of direct hits rocked the ship.

"Three of our engines are out, and the helm's not responding," Cartwright reported.

There were a dozen more bangs, and a dozen more thuds. With each one, the entire ship would rattle and roll.

"That can't be offal. What the hell is he shooting at us?"

The answer came a moment later when the detached head of an ox shattered a window and became wedged in its frame. His snout had come to rest mere inches from yours truly's and he looked as surprised to see me as I was to see him.

Then three more windows were taken out by the heads of a hog, sheep, and goat, respectively.

"Any suggestions, Horatio?"

"Yes. Pray like hell Lafitte is in a good mood. But I don't think that's very likely."

With no options, I ordered Cartwright to strike the colors and retired to my cabin for a quick swig of brandy. When I returned, three of the crew took me in hand, while Woese held a blade against my throat.

"Sorry, Captain, but looks like we got to play the mutiny gambit again," Blight told me.

"This time I'll have Horatio to back me up. At least he knows the meaning of loyalty."

"Me? I'm a free-lance." He licked a finger and held it

up. "I feel a change of loyalty comin' on."

Meanwhile, the pirate had maneuvered his ship within fifty feet of ours. This was made easier by the lines they'd attached to the severed heads. They sent a sort of footbridge out over one of the lines, and soon a dozen of their men had boarded through the window the goat's head had cleared for them.

"Who's captain?" one of the smaller among them asked. Like them all, he was dressed colorfully, with a long earring hanging from one ear, and a necklace of what appeared to be human bones.

"That would be me. I insist you take me at once to your captain so we can parley."

"Yeah?" He looked about the room. "Hey, Horatio. What are you doing with this mug?"

"You know me, Jack. I only work when I need money. And he had the money when I needed it."

"Mattie here?"

"Yeah, she's here...."

"Ah, Captain Tigue, I presume." I held out my hand, and Woese lowered his cutlass.

"What's going on?" Tigue asked, ignoring my gesture.

"My crew's putting on a little performance, pretending to have mutinied. In hopes you'll show them clemency."

"Clemency? I don't even know what the hell that means."

"Means you show us mercy, on account of us being forced to follow the orders of a ruthless—"

"Put a sock in it. And drop the blade. What's the poop, Horatio?"

"Well, I think the fellows are just having a little joke.

Worked for them back in Nassau, so why not try it again?"

"Well, joke's on them. The ship's yours, mister—good luck to you. Now let's get out of here. Smells like a New Orleans flophouse. Horatio, take Mattie and your captain to the *Goose*. The rest of you can go on your way."

"That ain't right, Cap'n Tigue," Albertson told him. "Can't you at least throw us a towline, 'til we get to port?"

"I don't make too many ports of call. I could use some galley slaves, if you want the job. Three meals a day, sunny days off."

"What kind of offer is that?"

"Best you're going to get."

II

The entire company took up Tigue's invitation and one by one we crossed the rope bridge over to his airship. *The Buttered Goose* was a massive craft, which made its name all the more incongruous. As soon as we'd boarded, the pirate chief insisted we all be given a thorough steam-cleaning. Afterward, the men were sent God knows where, and I brought to Tigue's cabin.

I never saw his sleeping quarters, but the ante-chamber impressed me greatly. It was done up like a rich man's study—carved oak paneling, oversized furniture, objets d'art, exotic curios, etc. All very lavish and, for the most part, within the bounds of good taste.

I hadn't noticed at our first meeting—perhaps too distracted by the knife at my throat—but he bore a strik-ing resemblance to Noyes Congdon: about the same height, five-six or so, sandy hair, blue eyes, and identical facial features. His customary expression, however, was quite unlike the maudlin millionaire's. Tigue wore a permanent half-smile, the insignia of the satisfied cynic, a man who finds mild amusement in all about him. In manner, too, he was the opposite of Congdon: cool to a point just short of somnolent.

"Wonderful to make your acquaintance," I told him, while giving him a second opportunity to forgo shaking my hand. "I believe we have a mutual friend, Clarisse... I'm afraid I didn't catch her surname."

"Me either. Sit down."

"Thank you. Say, I hope our little encounter didn't inconvenience you too much."

"No, not too much. Just so we can reuse the heads. They ain't easy to come by—and only get better with age."

"Good. And sorry about the offal. Not my idea, really. Came with the ship. Queer old thing."

"What's wrong with her?"

"Well, the name says it all: *Lucy's Revenge*."

"You don't like it?"

"Apparently Lucy was a lady of pleasure."

"Yeah. I named it myself."

"Oh. Well, it's very witty, of course."

"Christ, ain't you the soft-soap artiste? Forget *Lucy*—what was the big idea?"

"Well, it's rather embarrassing. A little error on my part. See, back in Tortuga, while I dined with... well, while I was occupied... that unpleasant Lafitte bird showed up and took prisoner one of my crew. And, for various reasons, I'm anxious to get her back."

"Her?"

"Yes, her—but boyish. Knows how to swear... and wield a razor, things like that.... Anyway, he made off with her and I thought I'd lie in wait and ambush him. I also believe he may have abducted my wife."

"Funny you didn't mention her first."

"Yes, I suppose it does seem odd. But in the first case, I'm certain Lafitte has the girl. With my wife... I don't suppose you might have raided the steamship *Paris*? Seventeenth of April, a Wednesday, I believe, in case that's any help."

"Nah. What'd they get?"

"Well, girls, mostly. And the usual wallets, watches, etc. But girls seemed to hold top spot on their shopping list."

"Well, I suppose that could've been Lafitte. Never heard of him taking on an ocean liner, though."

"And a real one, at that."

"What do you mean, a real one?"

"Oh... just that it was very large." I imagine it's unlikely people living in a fictional world are aware of their tenuous status. "Does Lafitte have any females among his crew?"

"I very much doubt it." He seemed to find the idea amusing. "Why?"

"Well, that press-gang that boarded the *Paris*—they were masked, but I have a suspicion they may have been women."

"Yeah?"

"Yes. The way they moved. Things like that."

"Huh. That's interesting.... But let's concentrate on Lafitte for now. How determined are you to take him on? He's a mighty tough egg, you know—with or without girls on his crew."

"Oh, pretty determined... within limits, of course."

"Well, reason I ask is that I'm planning on paying

him a visit. A certain friend of mine's gone missing, and I think he might have her."

"Seems to make a habit of abducting women."

"Yeah."

"What's his usual way of dealing with them?"

"He holds 'em for ransom."

"And if the other party is short of funds?"

"Auction."

"Oh.... Could be worse, I suppose."

"I suppose."

"When you say you're planning a visit, you mean to his base, in the bayous?"

"Yeah. Barataria."

"What sort of place is it?"

"Like Tortuga, only not so genteel."

"I see. And most everyone there is in Jean Lafitte's employ?"

"His or his brother's."

"What's the brother like?"

"Name's Pierre. He prefers to keep his dogs on terra firma, but otherwise just as disagreeable as Jean."

"I see. How many men are they likely to have?"

"A couple hundred. Maybe more."

"And how many do you have?"

"Including your crew? 'Bout forty."

"Do you mean you run this huge ship with just a couple dozen men?"

"Yeah. Most of that space is storage, then there's things like the handball courts, the sauna, you know. The secret's in staying organized. Anyway, you think it over."

"What's my alternative?"

"I maroon you in a dinghy with a half-pint of water."

"With or without a frying pan?"

"Sorry, can't spare one."

"Then I accept your proposal unreservedly."

"How about your crew?"

"I suggest we tell them that we're raiding a rum-runner's retreat, and leave off talk of the Lafitte brothers and their unpleasant nature."

When we parted, I was taken to my own quarters—a merely serviceable cabin, but provisioned with a very serviceable sherry. After a brief knock, Horatio entered carrying a tuxedo on a hanger.

"Dinner's at eight, cocktails at seven on the saloon deck."

"That's very civilized."

"Oh, Jack is very civilized."

"Odd, isn't it? I mean, an orphan who runs away to the circus..."

"How'd you know Jack was an orphan? Or about the circus?"

"Oh.... I believe Clarisse may have mentioned it. Of course, strictly speaking, he wasn't really an orphan. Turns out his father—"

"Whatever you do, don't mention Jack's father!"

"A sensitive point? Oh, yes, I remember. Miserable bastard. Railroad cop, wasn't he?"

"How do you know so much? No one knows that. You a crystal-gazer?"

"No, but I have a cousin who thinks she is. Of course, she's thoroughly insane...."

"They make the best seers. Mattie is a seer."

"Ah." I left it at that. "Will I see you at dinner?"

"No. I won't wear Jack's monkey suit. And Mattie, she doesn't like Jack's friends."

"Pretty crude?"

"No, that's the one thing they're not."

The elevator up to the saloon deck operated on a steam-powered piston, which I easily deduced on entering it. A sweltering cloud engulfed me as the cab rose through the twenty-odd intervening decks. I arrived looking as if I'd traveled by way of the Congo. I suppose all technological advances come with their drawbacks.

The saloon itself was refreshingly well ventilated and tastefully lit with just the minimal number of candles necessary, the light falling subtly on the oak-paneled walls and the walnut table. It was set formally for a party of eight. A steward in a white jacket approached me.

"Good evening, sir. The captain should be up shortly. In the meantime, might I interest you in a cocktail?"

"Martini, thank you."

I followed him to a sideboard where he expertly mixed my drink. He plopped in an olive and handed it to me. "You'll find the other guests on the balcony."

III

I went in the direction of his nod and found there was indeed a balcony—not a common feature on an airship. Of course, neither is a steam-powered elevator. There were six others already in attendance, some seated, some standing. The view was of the sun setting out over the Gulf, and the ship seemed to be oriented to maximize the effect. The view on the balcony itself was equally awe-inspiring: six shapely females, all dressed to advantage, and all worthy of attentiveness.

The four younger ones were standing in a small clutch near the rail so as to better admire the sunset. One or another was always shifting her feet and I spent a moment or two just watching their round bottoms bob like boats at anchor. Lest I become mesmerized, I strolled up to a tactful distance on their starboard and waited for an opportunity to insinuate myself into their conversation. The girl nearest me—a sultry blonde—wore a diminutive green dress that covered her behind barely and her back not at all. She had a delightful way of flouncing her bobbed mop when she laughed, leaning her head ever nearer mine. I took that as a signal and sidled closer.

They spoke to each other in whispers, and so quietly I couldn't make out a word. I'd need to take matters in hand.

"Simply exquisite," I said to the view, but when the sultry blonde turned toward me, I made clear my meaning. Too clear, perhaps. A sort of disgusted look came over her, as if she'd had a whiff of our ammunition. She surveyed me up and down, wearing the same expression, then turned back to her friends. I wasn't pleased at being cold-shouldered; what made it worse, she looked every bit as tempting from the front as from the rear.

A soft laugh came from the table shared by the two older women. When I say older, I'm speaking only relatively; neither could have been much over thirty. And though one was knitting, she didn't look remotely matronly. She smiled at me, so I went over and asked to join them.

"Oh, please," she said. She too was blonde, but wore hers a little longer than current style. It curved around her face and offered an apt frame for her arresting features. Her blue eyes sparkled, and her affable mouth seemed to move with her thoughts. "I'm afraid you won't have much luck with them. All under Captain Jack's spell."

"All thoroughly besotted," the other woman said, between sips of her highball. She was English, apparently, a redhead, whose curly hair fell about her shoulders in an unruly cascade. Her face was full and round, and yet she still managed to look stern. Not a classic beauty by any means, but one could sense a fire burning not far beneath the cold-steel shell. "Who are you?"

"My name is Van Slyke, erstwhile captain of *Lucy's Revenge*."

"Jack's old ship," the first woman noted. "I remember her."

"Yes, that's right. I acquired her just a couple days ago in Nassau."

"Are we to call you Van?" the redhead inquired.

"Well, since you asked, my full name is E. Pluribus Van Slyke."

"Is that a joke?"

"You'd think so, wouldn't you? Unfortunately, it was no joke to my father."

"So what do you go by?"

"Pluribus, generally, or Van Slyke."

"I think I'll call you E. Means 'out of,' doesn't it? What are you out of, Pluribus?"

"At the moment, Martini." I showed her my glass.

"Stanley," she called to the steward. "Might we have another round? And perhaps one for the nursery as well."

"Celia!" the blonde chided her. "Don't start anything in front of our guest...."

The only indication that the younger women had heard was a brief look back from a buxom brunette wearing entirely too much makeup.

"Sorry, Elissa," the redhead told her table companion. The contrition sounded genuine. "I suppose you know about our little family, Pluribus?"

"No, I only met Jack this afternoon."

"Well, now you've met Jack's harem."

I glanced at Elissa to see how she reacted to the word—she didn't look up from her knitting.

"You're not shocked, are you?" Celia went on. "After all, this *is* the 1920s."

"Well, I've seen quite a lot over the last few days that might have shocked me a week ago. I think I'm past shocking for the moment. Though I must admit I'm curious. Are there eunuchs guarding the doors?"

"No need. See, we're *all* besotted. With the possible exception of Elissa here."

"No," the blonde corrected. "I'm afraid I'm no exception."

"Do you mind my asking how you... Well, how does one go about enlisting in a harem?"

"In most instances, Jack saved us from some unpleasantness. In my case it was an abusive husband."

"Jack offered to take you away if you joined his harem?"

"Oh, no. At first, he merely confronted my husband."

"What did he say to him?"

"Nothing. Nothing at all—Jack eviscerated him. Well, you can see why I fell so hard for him."

"Oh, yes. Very obliging fellow. So Jack's quite the knight-errant?"

"Well, that's more a hobby than a vocation. He minds the store, you can be sure of that. But if time allows... Let's see, the little blonde who snubbed you... What's her name, Elissa?"

"Sue."

"Yes, Sue. Jack rescued her from a rival pirate, Jean

Lafitte. The one next to her, the one who looks like a trollop-for-hire, Betty-Ann, Jack rescued from a rum-runner. She claims to have been kidnapped, but... Next to her is Lena. Her case is analogous to mine, only with her it was an abusive father."

"Eviscerated?"

"Yes, I'm afraid Jack's a creature of habit. Then last, the little cutie with the black bob, Sheila—I'm not sure she could be considered a rescue, strictly speaking. She was wanting to make a call on a pay telephone and found herself without any coins. Jack noticed her plight and, without prompting, gave her a nickel."

"Not quite on the same scale as eviscerating an abusive husband."

"No, one wouldn't think so. But she says in New Jersey, where she's from, the two are about as likely."

"Yes. I've lived in New Jersey. There's much to what she says. But doesn't the arrangement create some inevitable friction?"

"Yes, of course. That's why there are no sharp knives at table. We dine mainly on seafood, and fricassees, things like that."

"And generally, women don't mind... a respite," Elissa added.

"What about the competition to bear Jack an heir?" I asked her.

She didn't respond, just set down her knitting and rose from the table. "I'll go see that things are ready."

Celia watched her walk inside. "Poor Elissa."

"Is she... unable?"

"Can't say. It would seem to be Jack.... But I shouldn't be telling tales out of school. Anyway, she's the only one who minds."

There was a laugh in the saloon, and the four girls at the rail all turned about. It was Jack. As he passed us, he nodded at me and winked at my companion, then disappeared, engulfed by the nursery.

"There's another benefit of the arrangement," Celia said. "If you're feeling morose you can sit back and enjoy it, and not have to put on a happy face for the contentment of your lord and master."

"Are you feeling morose?"

"Oh, I'm afraid it might be congenital. But it suits me, don't you think?"

"No, not particularly. Do you ever think of leaving?"

"Yes, but not yet. It may sound ridiculous, but this is the cheeriest home I've had."

"Not ridiculous at all. Still..."

The steward rang a little bell and we led the way to the table. Once all seated, we went quiet and Betty-Ann—the painted trollop—recited a simple prayer she no doubt remembered from childhood. The others made perfunctory shows of folding their hands and mouthing the words. Simply to humor Betty-Ann, I gathered.

Compared to the fare one imagines served aboard Blackbeard's ship, the meal was a light one. There were no whole hogs or legs of mutton. Clams on the half shell to start, then a salad of greens and various exotic fruits. Then sea bass, in a sauce that was creamy yet unusually flavorsome. I thought I detected almond, but it was too complex to identify ingredients. With it came asparagus sautéed in garlic. The next course consisted of shredded chicken in a sauce of chocolate and chiles, a Mexican dish they called mole. Last came a small dish of sorbet.

Various mediocre wines were served—his cellar was the one area Jack failed to measure up. And though a wide assortment of tableware lay before us, there were indeed no sharp knives. In fact, no knives of any sort.

I answered what questions came my way, but remained guarded in my answers, putting the best gloss possible on my naval career. The conversation amongst them stayed civil, even friendly. But there were occasional remarks—their meaning indecipherable to me—which brought a rise in tensions. These were usually smoothed over by Elissa asking one of the younger women some question. All four were simple girls, of limited experience and learning. But she would manage to find some topic—like asking Sheila to describe Atlantic City—which allowed the girl to wax on, much to the entertainment of the others and, not incidentally, to the bolstering of her own self-esteem.

Celia was the odd woman out. She couldn't bring herself to humor others. But she was also the one Jack watched most often. They teased each other with little remarks that flew above the heads of the younger girls.

It was an unorthodox family, all right. But I'd seen few more contented ones. Elissa had her disappointment to contend with, but who among us doesn't? And hers wouldn't have been solved by having Jack to herself. Celia, I imagined, would be equally morose with or without exclusivity. Though perhaps not before having met the husband who Jack had gutted on her behalf.

IV

After dinner, the six women took turns reading aloud. The book was *Robinson Crusoe*. The younger girls often—and Elissa occasionally—tripped over words or phrases. Oddly, it was Celia who came to their aid. She patiently explained pronunciations and provided definitions for obscure and archaic words. It was almost midnight when Jack interrupted.

"We gotta stop there. Our guest and I have some details to work out. And no going on without me!"

Once we'd entered the elevator, he asked me what I thought of his flock.

"Well, I can certainly see the attraction...."

"Hell, it's hard work. I'd like nothing better than to get 'em all married off."

"Even Elissa?"

"Especially Elissa. She should be in some small town, married to a banker."

"Oh, no, not a banker. How about a lawyer? Bankers and I never seem to get along."

"I'm the same way with lawyers."

"Well, then, how about a prosperous farmer?"

"Christ, no. Comes in after fourteen hours in the fields...."

"Good point. Well, a prosperous merchant. Owns the town's only store dealing in fine ladies' garments."

"Yeah. I like that...."

When we reached his cabin, he poured me a cognac.

"Just got that off a boat headed for Devil's Island. Must be the warders there live high. Well, bottoms up."

Cognac is a drink best appreciated by the sip, but Jack wasn't the sort who did things by half-measures.

"Here's the plan. I'm sending the *Goose* on to Kansas City. Me, you, and your crew will take *Lucy* to Barataria."

"Oh. So none of your men at all?"

"No. I figure it's better this way. The *Goose* would stick out like a sore thumb. And your men won't be recognized there. They'll think you're just another rum-runner coming to port. We'll load a few crates of rotgut to make it plausible. And I'll need to lay low."

"But you *are* coming?"

"Sure, I'll be there. But there's money to be made in Kansas City if I can get the goods there now. That's why I'm sending the *Goose* on."

"I didn't realize Kansas City was such a wet metropolis."

"It's dry as a bone. See, I've developed this system, me and an associate working on the ground. He's a federal agent, with the Prohibition force. He finds out where all the speaks in a town get their hooch. Then while he busts up the speaks and bootleggers, I take out the rum-runners and cut off supplies. I was only down in Tortuga looking for that friend I told you about."

"And looking in on Clarisse...."

"Oh, well, I'd missed her last time around. Anyway, this Kansas City operation has been going on for a couple of months now. A bottle of Scotch there would probably set you back a couple C's."

"And the *Goose*'s holds are full...."

"Exactly."

"Well, if ever you find yourself in need of help..."

"After you get your wife back, of course...."

"Yes, of course." Given Jack's thoroughness in dealing with husbands he found inadequate, I didn't wish to fall short of the mark.

"We'll need to make way by four. Better get what sleep you can."

"All right. Good night, Jack."

"Night."

Feeling that Jack's revised plan made the ill-starred

mission appreciably more ill-starred, I didn't expect to be getting much sleep. Then I entered my cabin and I forgot about sleep altogether. Celia was there going through my meager belongings. She looked only mildly surprised to see me.

"Spying in Jack's service?"

"Oh, you can be sure he's already taken care of that. I just wanted to satisfy my own curiosity."

"Have you?"

"No, not really. Are you really in the American Navy?"

"Well, that depends how you define *in*. I was *in*, as in on the rolls, up until a couple years ago. Now I'm more on or about than in, a sort of privateer.... Like your own Sir Francis Drake."

"I see. Just looking for an armada to vanquish?"

"Yes. Unfortunately there don't seem any about."

She shook her head, but she smiled as she did.

"Where are you from?" she asked. "You don't speak like the average American. Canadian? Or patrician by birth?"

"No, pure affectation, I'm afraid." Now she laughed. A little laugh, but a laugh nonetheless. "I was born on a subsistence farm on a rocky hill in Massachusetts. My mother died when I was an infant, and my father when I was nine."

"Sounds tough. And then off to the Dickensian workhouse?"

"Not as bad as that. But the circumstances made me determined to better myself.... Or, failing that, to get the better of others."

She laughed her little laugh again. "You *are* something else." She nodded at my ring finger. "How long have you been married?"

"Married? Oh, less than a year. It's partly due to my wife that I'm on this quest. Regrettably, she's been kidnapped. On the high seas."

"Are you serious?"

"Perfectly. Pirates, of one ilk or another, attacked the liner we were on. It's my search for her that led me to Tortuga, and to my misguided assault on Jack." This line of conversation was unlikely to work in my favor. "But that's been resolved, thankfully. Tell me about you... before you married."

"Not much to tell," she said, then spent the next hour telling me.

In a nutshell, she grew up as an only child in a middle-class household with a distant mother and an attentive, but overly strict, father. Marrying her ne'er-do-well husband was her pivotal act of rebellion.

"Have you considered going back to your parents now? Perhaps they have their regrets as well."

"Too late for that. They're both dead and buried."

She looked even more morose than normal now, so another change of topic seemed in order. "I take it reading *Robinson Crusoe* was your idea?"

"Yes. When I joined up, Jack was having them read Yeats, and other, lesser poets of the Celtic Revival. Not to my liking, but must have appealed to his romantic outlook."

"Is Jack a romantic?"

"Oh, hopelessly. Anyway, I got him to try *Treasure Island,* with its pirates and adventure. Right up his alley...."

She was clearly more interested in talking than lovemaking, but eventually her tongue tired.

I'd been right about the fire burning not far beneath

the cold-steel shell; it just lay a little deeper than I suspected. She responded to my kisses, but not without a certain detachment, and seemed nearly indifferent to caressing, petting, and fondling. But within a minute of my going to work below decks, there wasn't the slightest trace of the cold-steel shell. She began whispering what sounded like lines of verse. Her pelvis she let lie helpfully stationary, but her legs twitched in a steady rhythmic pattern. First a quick shudder of the right, then a more protracted one of the left. Five times it repeated, then a quick inhalation and another line of verse accompanied by another round of tremoring thighs. It wasn't until I recognized some lines as coming from Shakespeare that I realized her legs were twitching in iambic pentameter. Eventually, she left off the poesy and raced through a succession of wordless trochees, spondees, and dactyls.

She pulled me up and seemed not at all disappointed that the final round wouldn't have made it through even one of Clarisse's courses. As we lay in each other's arms, she complimented my attention to detail.

"I've never experienced anything quite like *that* before...."

"You mean...?"

"Yes. I guess I've led too conventional a life." She giggled now like a girl.

"I would have thought Jack..."

"Oh, Jack has his... own way. He prefers we keep it a secret."

"Now you've *got* to tell me...."

She giggled again, then brought her mouth to my ear and whispered, "Jack has—"

CHAPTER 9.

LAFITTE'S MANICURE

"Up and at 'em!" Jack had let himself in. "Christ, not even dressed yet? Hey, Celia. Tell the others I'm going on a business trip with this bimbo. I'll meet up with you in a day or two."

He didn't seem the least bit surprised to see her in bed with me. I've read that Eskimos will share their wives with houseguests—though I've always assumed it's as often as not the wife's idea, it all depending on the houseguest in question. Who was behind Celia's visit I'd never know. Nor did I care, really—just so it was *her* behind doing the visiting.

"Yes, all right, Jack," she told him.

"You got five minutes," he said to me. He was dressed in a billowy fuchsia silk shirt over black trousers that went no further than his knees—what the smart pirate was wearing that season, I gathered.

By the time the door had clicked shut, I was already out of bed and dressing.

"Interesting guy, your Jack," I told her.

"Yes. Full of surprises. I nearly wet the bed."

"Care to finish what you were telling me?"

"Oh..." She looked at the closed door as if she wasn't quite sure Jack hadn't remained on the other side. "Not just now.... Anyway, good luck. I mean, finding your wife."

I looked down at her, holding the sheet about her not insubstantial chest, her rosy cheeks glowing amid the cascade of red curls.... Apparently she read my thoughts.

"I said, *good luck finding your wife.*"

"Yes.... You know..."

"I don't know.... Or at least if I'd believe you.... But thank you for saying so just the same."

I gave her my most sincere wink and went off.

Lucy had been serviced in the hours since Jack's ravagement of her. Her blown portals had been glazed anew and she'd been graced with a scent which nearly masked that of the unpleasant effluent she'd expelled during her recent struggle. At least until Albertson came aboard. No amount of steam-cleaning could render him agreeable.

In truth, the whole crew seemed in an ugly mood. If one had a barometer measuring their disposition, the needle would only rarely budge off "Foul" even in the best of times. But today it was something worse. Which seemed odd, since the expedition was saving them a few hours slaving at Jack's oars. I mentioned this to Cartwright.

"Well, see, Jack's ship operates on a different principle. First thing you got to understand is, the rowing of oars ain't so much rowing, as just working. It don't matter how the work gets done."

"So Jack uses some other means. Mules turning a crank?"

"No. Sport."

"Sport?"

"Boxing, mostly. There's some ball courts, but mostly it's fights."

There're few things seamen enjoy more than beating senseless their comrades, but I couldn't see how that translated into energy to make steam. Cartwright hadn't considered the question, and when I asked Jack about it, I received a similar answer.

"I don't know the nuts and bolts of it—something

about rising internal temperatures relative to external temperatures relative to something else. One of the steamfitters rigged it up. Told me it'd be better not to ask too many questions."

"I see." What I saw was further proof of Cousin Emmie's authorship. She couldn't be bothered dotting her i's and crossing her t's when it came to principles of thermodynamics.

"By the way, Jack, I haven't seen Horatio. Is he aboard?"

"I thought bringing him along on this mission might be a little chancy."

"I see what you mean—a negro making mischief in the deep South."

"Well, pirates and rum-runners ain't particularly opinionated in that regard. No, I meant chancy for me. See, if I came back without her Horatio, Mattie'd pierce my gut first chance she got."

"What finer mark of devotion could a woman show?"

"Yeah."

We were still running alongside *The Buttered Goose* at this point. But once we crossed the Louisiana coast, that ship continued to the northwest and we turned due north. Now Jack addressed the crew.

"Here's the plan. You'll anchor just outside Barataria, makin' sure you leave a few men to guard the ship. The rest go into town. Tell anyone that asks you're here to trade your rum. Lafitte's place is on a hill near the edge of town. There's a bar right next to it called the Stupid Pelican. Make your way there—but by ones and twos. When you get there, mill about. Don't hang around together. And try to stay reasonably sober. When it's time to strike, I'll get word to your captain. Any questions?"

"What's reasonably sober?" Albertson asked.

"Sober enough to beat off Lafitte's guards and rescue any women he's holding."

"I don't fight too good sober...."

"Well, sober enough to walk. How's that?"

"All right, I guess.... Do we get to keep the women?"

"If any will have you."

"Where are you going, Cap'n Jack?" Blight asked.

"To get the lay of the land and make some arrangements. I got a contact."

"Can I go with you?"

"Me too," Woese added.

"No. You'd queer the deal. Just be ready to follow your captain's orders."

"Oh, don't leave us with him!"

"Jesus!" Jack turned to me. "Where'd you pick up these he-men? A convent school?"

"The brig, most of them. I'm not sure they're adequately inured to battling pirates just yet."

"*Adequately inured?*"

"Prepared. Maybe we should delay the operation until after they're ready?"

"Nit. It's now or never."

"Never'd suit me," Albertson told him.

"What do you think our odds are?" Cartwright asked.

"Of dyin'? Ten out of ten if you don't do just what I tell you to. And don't think of changing colors. If Lafitte finds out you came here with me, he'll slit your throats and feed you to his hogs."

The secret to successful pirating seemed to lie in the imagery one projected.

We brought *Lucy* down to seventy-five feet and Jack repelled to the mangroves below. His little speech hadn't steeled the men's will, but at least his threat quelled any thoughts of insurrection. Frankly, my will needed some shoring up as well. The memory of the bounteous redhead I'd left lying in that comfortable bed was hard to shake.

But shake it I must.... I forced my thoughts upon Aggie, recalling her girlish form, and the gratifying way she'd trembled when my hand brushed across her nipple. She was down there in Lafitte's Bastille, in desperate need of aid. And possibly Sesbania as well—whose nipples were nearly as responsive.

An hour later, we moored *Lucy* to a tall pine near three other ships similarly anchored. Next we put a healthy dent in the rum Jack had supplied us with as bait. Entering a pirate haven sober, I reasoned, would cast a good deal of suspicion on us. And we were all in need of some encouragement.

I left three men behind, none of whom had any idea how to run the ship, and only one still sober enough to stand. They might not be much use as guards, but at least they weren't capable of stealing off before our return.

Albertson I kept close at hand. He'd been seen by Lafitte, but I hoped we could take advantage of his resemblance to the pirate's second-in-command. I directed the men to refer to him as Geoff l'Indigné, which left them confused no matter how painstakingly I explained it. And none more so than Albertson himself.

Just as Jack had instructed, we entered town in ones and twos and made our way to *Le Pélican Stupéfait*. I should note, the name properly translated to the Stupefied Pelican, which described the bird on the signage to a tee. The pirate standing behind it seemed to be in the opening round of the sport depicted at *Le Pélican Débauché*. This keenness for the bird among pirates struck me as disturbing, but I'd venture not nearly so disturbing as the pelicans themselves found it.

Out of twelve men in the away party, six managed to make it to the bar—about as good as I dared hope. The saloon looked so similar to Clarisse's Pelican I wondered if she had a chain of such establishments, one at each of the principal pirate haunts. The depravities exhibited by the clientele also ran along similar lines, though the energy devoted to them was noticeably restrained. This I attributed to the fact it was only just ten in the morning.

I made a point of addressing Albertson as Geoff the moment we entered. But the indignation would require some convincing work on his part. I began goading him about his grooming. When he seemed slow to take the bait, I told him I'd seen his missing finger in a jar of pickled pig's knuckles at a barroom down the street. This new line worked to perfection. He picked me up and threw me into a table some yards away.

A little later—once I'd come to—he helped me off the floor.

"Well done," I whispered. "But you don't want to appear too solicitous."

He looked at me in total bewilderment. There was nothing odd in that. Bewilderment was Albertson's expression of both first and last resort. What did seem odd, however, was the way in which he responded.

"*Quoi?*" he asked, with a very credible accent. A simple bit of French, perhaps, but no doubt beyond Albertson's limited linguistic acumen.

I looked down at his left hand and counted the full complement of appendages. The small finger of his right hand, however, was conspicuous by its absence. I'd addressed my confidence to Geoff l'Indigné himself. I took some solace in the fact that he wasn't at that moment looking particularly indignant, but I soon learned that Geoff expressed himself mainly through his work.

"*Amenez-le au cachot!*"

Two of his henchmen grabbed me by the arms and shoved me along, out of the Pelican and into an alley. There they tossed me in a puddle of filth. Thinking that might be the end of it, I felt myself lucky. I'd been tossed in far fouler puddles than that.

But instead, it was just the beginning. They again picked me up and tossed me down a masonry stairway. It led to the basement of the large house next door, presumably Lafitte's manor. They dragged me into the faintly lit cellar, then forced me to lie down on what I'd normally call a very uncomfortable plank. However, compared to my dip in the cesspool, and the bouncing down the stone steps, it came as a relief. At least until they bound my wrists and ankles with cord.

My French is no more than serviceable. Hence I was unfamiliar with the term for the place to which Geoff had ordered his men to bring me. But now that my eyes had adjusted to the dimness, I was able to determine that *cachot* must translate to something along the lines of dungeon, or, more specifically, chamber of horrors.

I've always appreciated opportunities to expand my vocabulary. Nonetheless, I had difficulty taking much joy in this latest addition. There were any number of souls chained to the walls of the place. Mere skeletons, mostly. Some metaphorically, some quite actually. And the stench was overpowering. I suspected my dunking in the puddle was an attempt to freshen up the place.

Geoff joined us and issued various instructions to his men. They spoke in an Acadian patois, with most utterances punctuated by cackles. I had a hard time deciphering the pidgin French, but the cackles I read quite easily.

"I don't think you know what you're risking," I told him in his own language. "I'm an officer of the United States Navy. If harm comes to me, there will be grave repercussions."

Geoff found this particularly amusing. He sauntered over to one of the corpses lining the walls and removed the moth-eaten remains of an officer's hat. The moth-eaten remains of an officer's head came with it. The three of them were now in stitches. Geoff used the hat as a sling to send the flesh-shrouded skull along to one of his men. This man head-butted it to his co-henchman, who nimbly stepped out of the way, allowing the severed head to land in my lap. I looked down to see it staring back at me just as Geoff placed the hat on my own crown. More hysterical laughter.

Say what you want about pirates, few others take such a genuine pleasure in their work. The next bit of which involved wheeling over a large contraption that seemed to be some sort of steam-powered meat slicer. My right wrist was untied, then strapped to a round plate, with the fingers and thumb each individually tied into position. The machine took a while to start up, but once it did, I could see it incorporated three movements. The first sent a blade down a few inches from the tips of my digits. The second involved a pivot of the plate. And the third brought the blade ever closer to my fingers.

It looked as if they were to be sliced off one after another in half-inch increments.

II

When it became apparent to Geoff that I'd deduced the purpose of his diabolical machine, he fell silent and looked down upon me with a smile and raised brows, as if awaiting my tribute to the ingenuity of the thing.

"You blackguard! You'll pay in hell for this!" I didn't bother putting this in French. It seemed unlikely the response would have been anything beyond more cackles regardless.

Someone shouted down an interior stairway. Geoff looked mildly alarmed, then led his henchmen away. When he reached the top of the stairs, he sent me one last cackle before slamming the door closed.

The cord binding my ankles and left wrist had some give, so I began methodically testing each in turn. Meanwhile, the machine seemed to be ever quickening its pace. The knife fell with a sharp ping, the plate turned with a dull click, and a whoosh of steam announced another advance toward my fingers. I was becoming desperate. I cupped my left palm and yanked my arm with all my might. Now the machine was really whirring—*ping, click, whoosh, ping, click, whoosh....*

Suddenly, it dawned on me: my own struggle powered the means of my disfigurement! The sentiment behind this device of torture may have been pure pirate, but its tortured mechanics were all Cousin Emmie. And this opened up the possibility of exploiting her scientific illiteracy. All I needed to do was remain perfectly motionless. I did so and the machine slowed accordingly—*ping... click... whoosh... ping... click... whoosh....* When I reduced my breathing to once every thirty seconds, it came nearly to a stop.

But my condition remained dire. My best hope was that Jack would manage to defeat Lafitte with the help of my crew and free me along with the girls slated for auction. Until then, I needed to restrict my breathing and try not to wince every time the blade fell.

In the event, however, things proved not so simple. It probably comes as no surprise that pirates aren't zealous in their housekeeping. Cobwebs were everywhere, and a veritable sea of dust showed itself in the stray beams of light coming through the high windows. Soon my nose began to itch. Luckily, there was no possible way to scratch it and thereby speed the contraption. A moment later, however, I felt a sneeze coming on.... I managed to suppress it remarkably well—until someone opened the outside door and allowed a rush of air to churn up the dust....

The ensuing sneeze propelled the machine into its next cycle. Then another sneeze and another cycle.... The succession quickened—*sneeze, ping, click, whoosh, sneeze, ping, click, whoosh, sneeze, ping, click, whoosh*.... It wasn't now the dust tickling my nose, it was the bursts of steam themselves! This ingenious contraption had become a perpetual-motion means of torture. There'd be no stopping it now....

"All you gotta do is stay still!" It was Jack. "Hell, they had me strapped to the thing for three days once."

"I'd be more than happy to concede your supremacy in the sport if you'll just turn the damn thing off."

He fiddled with some levers, then some knobs, then, at my suggestion, flicked a large switch labeled *Marcher / Arrêter*—at last bringing the machine to a halt just as the blade handily trimmed the nail of my index finger.

"They call it Lafitte's manicure. Another minute and yours would have been permanent. Wouldn't kill you—"

"Maybe not, just the same…"

"You didn't let me finish. Wouldn't kill you *right away*. Take an hour or two for the loss of blood to finish the job."

"Perhaps you could untie me before going into further detail?"

"Sure." He took the cutlass from his belt and in three deft strokes freed my ankles, wrists, fingers, and thumb. "It looks like it's just you and me. Your crew musta hightailed it back to *Lucy* when they saw Geoff drag you away. Real dependable gang you got."

"They lack much, but they do have one quality."

"What's that?"

"A willingness to work for food and rum ration alone—just as long as you define work loosely. You aren't honestly proposing that you and I take on Lafitte's entire crew by ourselves?"

"Jean and most of his men are off pirating. Just his brother, Pierre, and a skeleton crew."

He noticed me looking about at my roommates.

"Not that skeleton…. But only a dozen or two men."

"Only a dozen or two? Including Geoff? Odds still seem a little long."

"I have some people creating a diversion. A raid on one of their warehouses. Geoff went off with most of the men. Can't be more than five or six upstairs guarding the women. Can you handle a sword?"

"I was on the fencing team at Annapolis."

"Yeah, what's that mean? As long as the other guy plays by the rules and uses a blade with a rubber tip?"

Given his insolent response, I chose not to divulge

my primary duty was to carry the team's water. I took the cutlass he offered and waved it about in the air. I don't think I impressed him. And especially not after the waving turned up the dust and brought on another bout of sneezing.

We crept upstairs, where Jack quietly opened the door. Or tried to. In addition to being lackadaisical about dusting, pirates are also negligent when it comes to oiling hinges. Instantly, two cutthroats were upon us. While Jack eviscerated the first, I manfully annoyed his comrade. Then Jack eviscerated him as well.

I hadn't quite believed Celia's account of her late husband's demise—but I did now. Jack was not just an efficient butcher, but a surprisingly neat one. The men's entrails fell in tidy heaps, and not a speck of blood besmirched his elegant ensemble. I, on the other hand, was quite thoroughly awash in the stuff.

"They usually lock the women up on the second floor."

"You've been here before?" I asked, wiping the sticky gore from my eyes. "On the same mission?"

"Sure. It's on my circuit."

Apparently, Jack was an efficient knight-errant as well.

Having found the back stairs obstructed by a wall of brick, he led me toward the front of the large house. It was a genuine antebellum mansion, with all the requisite carved woodwork, marble mantelpieces, and molded plaster ceilings. Not, however, in their original state. A hundred years of pirate habitation takes a toll on carved woodwork, marble mantelpieces, and molded plaster ceilings. The elegant freestanding stairway in the front hall reached only halfway up to the second floor. From that point on, one needed to pull oneself up a rope.

"You first," he said. "It's easy—go on."

I looked at him warily. But in fact I did find the going easy. The rope had been helpfully knotted every couple feet and this enabled the climber to push up with his legs. Less helpful was the hooligan up above. He was using a dagger to slice through the rope.

Jack let loose his own knife and the pirate fell to the floor twenty feet below.

"Hurry!" he rather gratuitously told me.

I managed to pull myself up, but no sooner had I made the landing than three more pirates appeared on the scene. I'd thought Geoff and his companions were laudable cacklers, but they had nothing on these three. It started in a choral chant, developed into a contrapuntal theme and variations, and ended with a finale in three-part harmony.

When I turned to suggest to Jack that he might likewise hurry, he was nowhere to be seen.

"I've come to offer you terms. I am an officer in the U.S. Navy, empowered by President Coolidge himself to offer full and unconditional pardons to whichever pirates assist in my mission."

"Prezident who?"

"Coolidge, of course."

"Never heard of heem. What iz your mission?"

"Monsieur Lafitte, I presume?"

"*Oui*. Pierre Lafitte." He stood only about five foot three, but was even more lavishly dressed than the others. All three made use of vast arrays of jewelry: gold rings, earrings, nose rings, and bangles, plus necklaces made of bone and teeth. The man to the left, however, took it a little too far. He was sporting what looked like a tiara. "I ask you again, what iz your mission?"

"Well... Some women were taken from a steamship back in April. I've been tasked with rescuing them."

They cackled a tune I recognized from the previous year's Ziegfeld Follies.

"Doesn't need to be all of them.... Let's say, a simple majority...."

This time it was the Introit from Mozart's *Requiem*. Impressive, but not a good sign, I suspected.

"There's really only one girl I'm particularly keen on. My wife, actually. About ye high. Brown eyes, chestnut hair. Mordant wit."

"Does zee have a mole on her bum?"

"Yes, she does, in fact...." I was glad of the confirmation, but the implications of his having that intelligence weren't lost on me. No one assaying her bum was likely to miss the goods above, or, for that matter, just around the corner. "Is she here?"

"Jean has taken her away."

"You wouldn't happen to know where?"

"Where zee will fetch dee highest price!"

In case I'd failed to grasp his meaning, they launched into a round of cackles, each in his turn trying to outdo the others, until Pierre ran a finger across his throat and all three went silent.

"Well, if the only way I can get her back is to win the bidding, I'm prepared to do that."

"Dee price will be paid in fine liquor—none of zis cheap rotgut."

"All right, that can be arranged."

"And dee winner must pay a buyer's premium of twenty percent."

"I happen to know fifteen percent is more usual, but

I'm flexible on that point. So where and when will the auction take place?"

"Zursday... Liquor an' choice comestibles on Tuesday; women an' fine dry goods on Zursday. Every other Saturday—"

Here he was cut short—figuratively, I mean. The man to his right, however, quite literally.

III

Jack had appeared from behind them.

He tossed me my sword and while he dispatched the third man, I finished off the ruffian he'd rendered legless a moment before. Pierre made no attempt to interfere.

"Well, you win again, Jack," he said gamely. "Lucky for you dese men are easy to replace, or I'd be angry." Jack knocked his hat off with his sword. "All right, all right. Don't be a ham. Just take dee girls and be gone!"

"Keys in the usual place?"

"Yes, yes."

While I tied up Pierre, Jack retrieved a set of keys from a nearby room. He led me down the hall and unlocked the first door we came to. It was inhabited by an impressive brunette wrapped in a kimono. As soon as the door opened, she draped herself over Jack.

"Oh, how... how can I ever repay you?" she asked, then she took a try at it by showering him with wet kisses.

Jack looked back at me and rolled his eyes. "You take the next one."

He tossed me the keys and I unlocked the second door. This girl hailed from the Far East, Chinese I'd guess. She had a classically round figure, a mesmerizing gaze, and a pouting mouth. I smiled reassuringly, then opened my arms to receive her. She stared at me suspiciously, inched herself away with her back to the wall, then leapt upon Jack. Now she too was showering him with wet kisses.

I went on to the third door and opened it. A woman who looked part Indian began cursing me in Spanish. It seemed she, too, took me for one of her jailers. When she saw the others attached to Jack, she joined in their efforts. By now he was one thoroughly sodden pirate.

Immediately behind the señorita came a parrot. There was nothing particularly noteworthy in this. After all, pirates and parrots go together like ham and eggs. But I didn't like the way this bird was looking at me.

"*Ah, ishkabibble,*" he squawked. "*Ain't I worked the theatrical beat?*"

I swung at him with my cutlass.

"*You don't know from cruel and ruthless, mister.*"

I swung again, nearly clipping a wing this time.

"Forget the damn bird!" Jack shouted. "Keep going, there's usually at least four...."

I'd just opened the last door when Albertson stumbled up behind me.

"I'm Injun Jeff!" he insisted. He was so utterly besotted he could barely stand. "Where the hell's my woman?"

"Please! No!" the female inside begged.

I'm not sure whether it will surprise you, but she looked the spitting image of Dorie, Congdon's scullery maid back on Long Island. Albertson apparently thought so too.

"Dorie?" he asked.

"Dottie," she corrected. "An' I'd slit my own throat before I'd let you..."

"Actually, we're here to rescue you," I told her. "You'll have to forgive Albertson. Had a little too much to drink."

"Ain't he Geoff l'Indigné?"

"No, just pretending to be."

She walked toward us, but with a pronounced limp. "My damn ankle. Tryin' to get away...."

Albertson surrendered his bluster and tenderly offered her a hand. When she accepted, he picked her up as if she were a kitten. Which was all the more astonishing since she outweighed him by fifty pounds at the very least.

"Come on, we better make tracks before the rest of them get back," Jack said, then led the way to the elevator both he and Albertson had evidently availed themselves of.

"Couldn't you have mentioned this was here before sending me up that rope?" I asked.

"Needed you to act as decoy."

I began to suspect my relationship with Jack would not prove as mutually satisfying as I'd hoped.

Back aboard *Lucy,* we took to the air and headed northwest in order to rendezvous with *The Buttered Goose*. While Jack attended to the other girls in my cabin, I interviewed Dottie in the galley. She sat devouring copious quantities of ham, eggs, and fried potatoes while we spoke. The display fell something short of ladylike, but my need for information was urgent.

I first asked about Sesbania, but she could only tell me that she might have been among Lafitte's captives.

"They didn't let us mix much, you know what I mean?"

"Yes, of course. I don't suppose you happen to know

where he's planning to hold his auction next week?"

"Somewhere north." A cascade of scrambled eggs slid down her chin. Albertson attentively wiped them away with a napkin and she continued. "Said he'd hit the rum-runners off of New York on his way."

"But you didn't get the name of the place?"

"Uh-uh."

The parrot flew into the room.

"He's got himself a cabin boy!"

I threw a hot cup of coffee at it, but it just hopped to the far side of the galley.

"Did you happen to see a girl Lafitte took aboard in Tortuga?" I asked Dottie. "Petite-sized. With bobbed dark hair and a caustic tongue. Traveled with this same parrot. Her name's Augusta Ready, though friends call her Aggie.... Wears a severed finger around her neck, if that's any help."

At mention of his finger, Albertson dropped a plate of pie he was bringing to the table.

"Yeah, she's aboard, too," Dottie said. "Only she ain't headed to the block."

"You think he'll kill her?"

"Kill her? Hell, no. He took a liking to her. It's on account of not gettin' along with her that Geoff l'Indigné got left behind."

A mere three hours later, Jack emerged. He looked winded.

"Christ, I'm gettin' too old for this business." I doubt he was over thirty, and seemed to be in excellent health. Which ought to give you some idea of the demands made upon him.

"Well, if you need some help with the females..."

"Hell, it ain't that easy. But speaking of females, I

found out where your wife is going to be auctioned. St. Pierre."

"Where's that?"

"An island off of Newfoundland. Part of a French holding, St. Pierre and Miquelon."

"Oh, yes. Well, we should be able to make it up there easily within a week. You are coming, aren't you?"

"Yeah. I'm still looking for that friend of mine. According to Elsbeth, she wasn't aboard Lafitte's ship. But he might have been holding her there already."

"Which one's Elsbeth?"

"The only one who speaks English. I don't suppose you know what *gèng duō* means in Chinese?"

"No, why?"

"It's all that comes out of Li Min's mouth. Girl's like a Celestial rabbit."

I was even more certain now that Jack and I could never be more than acquaintances.

"*Girl's like a Celestial rabbit,*" the parrot echoed.

I went in search of something to poison its feed with.

We spent that night and the next day in Kansas City while Jack wrapped up his business obligations and integrated the new girls into his harem. Sue, the little blonde I'd met previously, decided things had been competitive enough and went off to Chicago with Jack's blessing and a generous dowry. Betty-Ann, the pious painted trollop, objected to the ethnic impurity of the new class. She made plans to marry the charismatic host of a radio show she esteemed: a man of the cloth by day, and an Imperial Wizard of the Klan by night.

So it was really just a net gain of one for Jack's work load.

Horatio and Mattie rejoined us aboard *Lucy,* and

about five that afternoon the two ships set off together on a heading of east-northeast. The wind blew in our favor and we made excellent time. With little to do, the crew looked for diversion. Albertson took Dottie on a tour of the ship, no doubt hoping to find a secluded nook and there explore one or two of hers. Unfortunately—for him as well as the rest of us—they came across a calliope in a loft above the oar deck. Dottie sat down and gave the ship an impromptu concert. Her father was organ master at a Camden movie house, she later explained, and she'd picked up what she could from him. Apparently, that wasn't much. She treated us to thirteen aborted attempts at the overture to *William Tell*. When she finally stopped to take a break, I sent up Blight and Woese with a couple of axes.

The sun didn't set until after eight. By then we were somewhere over Illinois—assuming Cousin Emmie had placed Illinois in its usual spot. With the arrival of night, I ordered a detail of men to the oars. Their fondness for rowing, however, was no match for Jack's crew's fondness for pounding the life out of one another. We began to lag further and further behind, until our consort slipped from sight entirely. With nothing to do but hold our course, I turned the bridge over to Horatio and went to my cabin.

About an hour before dawn, I relieved him. He looked all in. But apparently mending came before sleep—keeping Horatio's buttons sewn on was a Sisyphean task, and not as quiet a one as you might think.

By then, it'd been five hours since we'd lost sight of the *Goose* and I'd nearly given up hope. But just ten minutes later, she reappeared a half-mile off our port bow. Not, however, alone. A second ship had engaged

Jack's in battle—this one even larger. He shot off his animal heads, but they didn't seem to be having the same efficacy they'd had against *Lucy*.

The opposing ship, all black as night, replied with something else entirely: goo. It came in semi-liquid splats, but appeared to harden quickly. One by one, the enemy gunners brought Jack's engines to a halt. Who this other ship belonged to was unknowable. Dottie, however, felt certain it wasn't Lafitte's.

I had two options, as I saw it: launch an almost certainly futile attack on the much larger craft, or leave the scene with all the speed we could muster. So, one option, really. I thought briefly of offering to take Jack's harem to safety, but I doubted any of them would abandon their savior in his moment of peril. Not even rosy-cheeked Celia. No, if I wanted a harem, I'd need to go about it myself.

I've a talent for rationalizing my less-than-heroic moments, but in this case, that was hardly necessary. After all, I was on a mission to save my supposed wife. *And* fulfilling an obligation to what passed for my president. Granted, she'd seemed less than distraught at being abducted; and he'd sent me off hoping I'd die in a fiery crash. But she was still my supposed wife and he was still what passed for my president.

Besides, given Jack's prowess with a cutlass, it wasn't beyond the realm of possibility he and his harem might escape a mortal end. And a lesser loss—say, an arm or a leg—might even do him some good. That smug self-assurance of his could stand to be taken down a limb or two.

Well, I don't know if that reasoning satisfied you, but it did me.

The damned parrot was another matter.

"Poor Jack Tigue! Deserted, and left for dead! Disgrace! Dishonor!"

I flung a pair of binoculars at his head and hit Cartwright's instead. But I made no apology. The bird must have been aping somebody, and as likely him as anyone.

Chapter 10.

Interlude on the Delaware

We made excellent time that day. The crew—as anxious as I was to flee the scene of battle—remained at the oars until well after sunrise. When Horatio emerged, I worried he might chide me for abandoning Jack. Instead, he once more licked a finger and held it up.

"When the wind is at our back, we must sail.... Time an' tide don't wait for no one.... Every man for himself, and the devil take the hindmost—and all that ballyhoo.... Now, what have we got for breakfast?"

While he went off for his meal, I referred to an old atlas I'd found aboard. Though wholly inadequate to the task, it was the only comprehensive collection of charts I had. I drew a plot of our approximate course and hoped for the best. As luck would have it, I was able to confirm our position when we passed through the dense smoke rising from Pittsburgh's furnaces early that afternoon.

Whether it was soot from those fires that brought about our engine trouble, I can't say. But it was shortly after that we heard the first of a long series of groans from the boiler room. For the first hour or two, we just ignored them. *Lucy* had been through a lot in her time and the old girl wasn't shy about voicing complaints. But by evening, we were running at half-speed. I sent Horatio up to investigate and a gang to man the oars.

It did no good. Then Horatio returned and explained why.

"Trouble's not with making steam. It's the pistons the steam drives. I think the rings are worn out."

"Don't we carry spares?"

"Carry spares? When everything is working fine? Sounds like a lotta trouble."

"Yes. Very bothersome," I agreed. Horatio had never met Cousin Emmie, but he was, evidently, a practitioner of her school of logic. "Well, we need to make port, somewhere with steam shops.... Say, a railroad yard. There must be dozens around New York. We'll head down there.... Ah, there *are* railroads, aren't there?"

"What a crazy question."

"Is that a yes, or a no?"

"Yes! How else would people get around on land? Horse and buggy?"

We were to the northwest of the city, just crossing the Delaware River. Its valley ran to the southeast, so I turned to run along it. Suddenly, the whole ship shuddered.

"I don't think *Lucy* likes that plan," Horatio said. "Not another inch, she says."

We were adrift. Without propulsion, the rudder and elevators were useless. I saw a town on the north bank of the river, but it looked too small to be of use. Then a much larger burg came into view.

"Odds are, there will be some yards there," I said.

"I see 'em," Cartwright reported. "Just five hundred yards off the port bow. An' there's a roundhouse! Must be shops there."

"Good. Now we just need to set down near the river."

This was a task much easier said than done. Without power, we could only wait until we drifted over a suitable spot and then descend as quickly as possible. The wind had been from the northwest, which worked in our favor.

But then came a powerful gust from due west. It lifted us out of the valley to the hills above it. I'd already begun our descent and now tried to reverse it. But it was too late. *Lucy* came down just below the crest of a hill. And she didn't do it gracefully.

We had little choice but to secure the ship as quickly as possible. Otherwise, the next gust would send her battering against the ridge. We tied lines to whatever we could find. Save for a windbreak nearby, there were few mature trees about, so I had the men drive stakes as well.

It was after seven in the evening, but still plenty light. I felt sure someone must have seen our descent. So rather than wander about aimlessly, we sat tight and waited for them to come to our aid.

The setting seemed unnervingly reminiscent. The land had been cleared for pasture, and just down from the ship, cows grazed. It reminded me a little of my childhood home. As if on cue, a boy and girl, each about ten, arrived to gawk at the stranded ship. Outside of her hair being in the mandatory bob, they appeared not unlike kids on my hilltop, exhibiting the customary hand-me-down clothes, sun-bronzed complexions, and shoeless feet (de rigueur for all days on which the temperature reached fifty degrees or more).

"This your land?" I asked.

"Yeah. What made you stop here? Break down?"

"Yes. And it's going to take some work to fix it. What's the town we passed in the valley? The one with the rail yards?"

"Port Jervis, prob'ly. Whattaya need rail yards for?"

"Parts for the steam pistons."

Woese approached. "You say Port Jervis?"

"That's right."

"You know the place?" I asked him.

"I grew up just a few hills up that way." He nodded to our northwest.

He began quizzing the kids with names. None were familiar to them.

Their father turned up and he too was unacquainted with Woese's people. His name was Kemp, and he struck me as the polar opposite of my own father. He had the appearance of a man who spent all day in the fields. An upright sort of fellow who looked you in the eye and, I'd wager, served on the school board. I asked if he had a wagon I could take into town in the morning. Sure, he said—then specified terms for the rental. Mr. Kemp wasn't the gullible sort of hill farmer you find in popular anecdotes.

Woese asked to accompany him down the hill. I made no objection, even expecting I'd never see him again. He wasn't a particularly enthusiastic crewman, or particularly useful one. And there wasn't much chance of preventing his departure with his kinfolk so nearby.

I slept that night under the stars. Just as I had any-time I could as a boy, when four of us shared a house not much bigger than my cabin aboard *Lucy*. My mother died before I'd left infancy and I was raised by my older sister. My father wasn't much use in that regard. He was the town ne'er-do-well, and that was the only thing he *did* do well.

Our farm had to be the rockiest, most ill-kept farm in the commonwealth. In fact, rocks were about all that sprouted in our fields. A limitless supply. Little else would grow under my father's management, our crops invariably coming up late and stunted. We usually had a clutch of chickens and a couple dozen sheep and goats.

But any cows or hogs we tried to keep would abandon us at the first opportunity—they aren't nearly as dumb as they look.

My old man had inherited the place from his father. Grandpa had been an itinerant tinker and part-time medicine man. The Van Slyke name was his adaptation. He'd been born a Slocum—but that name just didn't sell. While passing through the Hudson Valley, he came across a clan of Van Slykes and soon after had labels made for Dr. Van Slyke's Sure-Cure. He pasted these on bottles of whatever concoction came cheapest, the only qualification being an alcohol content of not less than forty percent.

He did well traveling the back roads of New York and New England, and thoroughly enjoyed leading the life of the nomad. But one day he met my grandmother and fell immediately under her spell. It's a tired cliché, I know, but in this case there must be some truth in it. No one in their right mind would have settled on that pile of rocks otherwise—even if the hen-house did come with her.

That was before the Civil War, 1850-something. He wasn't much of a farmer either, but the war drove up prices generally, and of wool particularly, so the family prospered for most of a decade. Then came the inevitable bust. His two daughters escaped—one with another medicine man, the other with a liquor salesman. Soon after that, both grandpa and grandma passed on. My father was only seventeen when he inherited the place, an age when most boys would have been anxious to get off that hill. But Pa never suffered unduly from ambition.

He worked it as well as he could for a few years, but spent an increasing share of his time chasing the daughters of his neighbors. In my mother's case, successfully. When the result became irrefutable, they were married. And seven months later the twins were born.

Gloria emerged first. Her name originated with the *Battle Hymn of the Republic*. As did her brother's, Hallelujah, which heralded the hoped-for heir arriving shortly after she did. Six years later, when I came along, they christened me Pluribus—the plural, or surplus, son. The initial "E" was added later simply because one expected it there.

I've been told my father had been a faithful husband. How true that is, I can't say. But one of my earliest memories is coming upon him and Mrs. Tilden in our so-called orchard. She sat mounted on a low branch of one of the ill-tamed apple trees, with her skirt and petticoat pulled up above her knees. And there he was, working with a diligence he rarely exhibited otherwise. It looked like a scene out of Bobbie Burns.

When I inquired later, he explained that Mrs. Tilden had been stung by a bee and he was applying a balm. There were, apparently, a good many hives in those hills, as my father could regularly be found applying balm to the wives of his neighbors.

Ironically—or perhaps not so ironically, depending on one's perspective—he himself died of multiple wasp stings a few weeks shy of my tenth birthday. My brother Hal found him lying in a brier that held no fewer than half a dozen paper nests. There was a dent on the back of his head, which the coroner attributed to his fall on being stricken—a little odd, since he'd been found face down. That the nests had been transported to the brier was obvious to anyone living in the country—ordinarily, wasp colonies don't get along with one another. But this, the coroner wisely announced, lay outside his province.

My father's death—a caution, I'm sure, to philander-
ers everywhere—came as a great blow to me personally.
I'd been blackmailing him since that episode in the
orchard with Mrs. Tilden. It didn't net me much mone-
tarily, but my needs were modest in those days.

Now orphans, the three of us were taken in by a wid-
owed aunt, Cousin Emmie's mother. A godsend for Hal,
who'd been sent to work in the nearby shoe factory at
fourteen. And for me, who'd likely as not have followed in
his footsteps—and never had the chance to study Latin.

II

I rose with the sun, and as soon as Horatio's mending had been attended to, we set about dismantling the
piston cylinders. It was filthy work, but until we had
them apart there would be no way of being sure what size
rings we needed.

We could see the rings were deeply worn. Removing
them, however, was another matter. It required a special
tool, Horatio told me. I didn't bother asking if we had one
in the tool kit, for the simple reason there was no tool kit.

"Well, I imagine those locomotive shops below will
have what we need."

"Sure. But what will you pay them with?" he asked.

"I've already thought of that. We'll offer tours of the
ship for ten cents a head. People in places like this are
always looking for entertainment. See for yourself."

I pointed toward a porthole. *Lucy* was leaning about
thirty degrees to starboard and through the glass we
could see a knot of rural folk gawking at the ship.

"We'll set it up like a side-show. For an extra nickel,

Dottie can tell her tale of abduction by and ultimate salvation from the desperate pirate, Jean Lafitte. Albertson can play a captured pirate—all he needs to do is strike fear in the women and children, and he's pretty good at that already. Perhaps Mattie could sew him an eye-patch."

"Mattie will be too busy."

"Just how many loose buttons have you got?"

"No. I mean, she'll be busy telling fortunes."

"Ah. I remember your mentioning she was a seer. That's excellent, we can charge two bits for that."

"All right, but as her manager, I insist she get one bit."

"Then better make it four bits."

"Yes, much better. And another four bits to see the Zombie of Port-au-Prince."

"You?"

"Sure. Spent two seasons with the circus, Polk's Great Show. That's where I met Jack. And Mattie. But I won't let her do no cooch show."

"Perfectly reasonable."

It all came off better than I expected. Dottie volunteered to do the cooch show before I'd even asked. Once an hour, she drew a curtain and any adult male (or passably developed adolescent) willing to fork over two bits would be treated to some very energetic bouncing of body parts. Keeping with the theme, she claimed it was the same dance she used to mesmerize the pirates and thereby dissuade them from attempts on her virtue. I didn't doubt the dissuading, but I'm not sure mesmerize was the right word for it.

A little later, Woese surprised me with his reappearance. He pulled me aside.

"Something real strange about this place."

"Didn't you find your people?"

"No. Found the hill, all right. And the boneyard at the bottom of it. But the names on the headstones was all wrong. Then I go up to our farm. Same house, same barn. I catch sight of my pa, headin' in from the cornfield. Only he weren't my pa. Different name, different limp, different wife, everything. Said they had a boy, but he lives in New York. Making it big in radio. They let me spend the night, and this morning I've been looking all over for someone who knows me. What the hell's goin' on?"

"How to explain it.... Do you remember that storm? The one that sent us to the Bahamas?"

"Sure, how couldn't I? Nearly killed us all."

"Well, I think it did more than that. I believe we may have crossed over into a sort of... parallel world."

"What the hell's that mean?"

"I'm not sure exactly. But suppose one day you woke up and it seemed as if you were in a story from *Capt. Billy's Whiz Bang*."

"This ain't like that. Women in *Capt. Billy* give it up at the drop of a hat."

"Yes, they do run unusually charitable. But try to set them aside for the moment. I just mean it's a world from a story...."

"Well, we should at least be able to pick the damn story."

I assured him I shared his sentiment, then sent him off to help with the show.

By early that afternoon, we'd made about forty-five dollars. I took that and went down to fetch Mr. Kemp's wagon. In addition to the fee agreed on earlier, he now insisted on some form of rental for the show grounds. I proposed free admission for him and his family. When he was slow to take up the offer, I threw in a private cooch show for him alone.

I had little trouble finding the Erie's roundhouse, and its chief engineer. He, unfortunately, was the typical sort of railroad functionary. So wedded to rules, regulations, and procedures, he'd make the most obstructionist bureaucrat blush. He told me he'd need to get approval from the general superintendent in New York.

"Should have an answer for you by late tomorrow."

"But can you at least tell me if you have the size of rings I'm looking for?"

"That's what I'm asking him, if it's OK to tell you whether or not we have them. If he says yes, we can ask the chief purchasing agent if it's all right to sell them to you."

I left him not in the best of moods. It would be simpler to take a train into New York and find what I needed there. But by then it was after three and there seemed no point in arriving after hours. I could just as easily catch an early-morning train and be back by the end of the day.

In the meantime, I stopped by the local library. I'd become curious as to which aspects of this make-believe world ran true and which didn't. For instance, the geography seemed essentially the same. And the Erie Railroad ran where it should. But what about people? From what Woese told me, that was a different matter.

I started with the New York dailies. The names of the newspapers were the same, but the personages they mentioned were all rechristened. The president of the United States answered to Clampett, not Coolidge—though admittedly the new moniker wasn't altogether inappropriate for Silent Cal. And while most of the cities and towns were recognizable, there was one place upstate called Byblos. That was the exception that proved the rule—a place name of Emmie's invention.

"Finding what you need?" the librarian asked.

I looked back at her dumbstruck. It was my high school Latin teacher. Only, she hadn't aged a day since that fateful afternoon when she'd allowed me to partake of her tutelage. Even more bizarre, she was smiling at me. And it looked to be a sincere smile, at that.

"Are you all right?" she asked.

"Sorry, for a brief moment I thought you were someone I knew. You wouldn't happen to have an older sister who teaches Latin?"

"No sister at all," she laughed, then bit her tongue to keep from laughing further.

To say I found the encounter arousing would be a supreme understatement. One of my recurring adolescent fantasies was to come upon my pedagogue in a playful mood. What's more, this librarian seemed to be reading my mind. I caught her staring down at my tightened trousers, biting off another incipient laugh. I couldn't help laughing myself.

"Shhh!" she cautioned impishly.

"I don't suppose you'd be free for dinner?"

"We're open late tonight. I don't get off until nine. Do you have something to do with that airship?"

"I'm its captain. How'd you guess that?"

"Just didn't seem to be from around here."

"Look, we're having a sort of open house. If you'd like a personal tour of the ship, I'd be happy to provide you one."

"Yes, I'm sure you would.… All right. It will probably be about ten that we'll get there."

"We? Bringing a friend?"

"A friend with a buggy. You wouldn't want me to walk all that way, would you?"

"No, certainly not. Wouldn't want you arriving winded.... Until ten."

I kissed her hand, theatrically, just so I could see her bite off another laugh. She did, then, as she turned, ran her pert little behind over my midsection. I believe she was gauging my fervor. She didn't find it wanting.

For a moment, I wondered if perhaps this *was* a story of Captain Billy's. Of course, he'd never have named a city Byblos. He was more the Sodom and Gomorrah type. That got me to thinking about Cousin Emmie. I stopped by the Erie's station and sent her a wire in Brooklyn; perhaps as fictioneer of this travesty, she might be reachable at her usual address. It read:

Have entered your world. Now how do I get back?

It occurred to me she might exist under a pen name, so I sent it to "The Author Residing at." For the return address, I put "Disabled Airship above Town (free cooch shows for messengers)."

Back outside, a little guy in grease-stained overalls sidled up beside me.

"You interested in makin' a deal?" he whispered.

"What sort of deal?"

"I work at the shops. Heard you talkin' to the chief."

"I see. Can you get the rings?"

"What size?"

"Seven-inch."

"Yeah, we have 'em. Five bucks per."

"Can't cost more than a dollar in New York."

"Prob'ly right. But you ain't in New York."

"All right. Three dozen. Plus the tools for mounting them."

"I'll need to bring those back before morning. ...And there'll be something for the rental."

"All right. Free cooch show for you and your friends."

"Deal. See you after dark, about nine."

I loaded the wagon with cartons of candy bars and Cracker Jack, and three kegs of root beer, then headed back up to the ship.

Business there was booming. The whole crew had gotten into the act. Blight and Woese had repaired the calliope they'd disabled two nights before and Horatio had hired a church organist who performed sinister-sounding pieces by Bach and his ilk. Meanwhile, the remainder of the crew had joined Albertson playing pirates—with the less gifted among them playing dead pirates. I borrowed a couple of the corpses and put them to work manning a concession stand.

My supplier showed up just after nine with the piston rings and an entourage of half a dozen inebriates insisting on their cooch show. Dottie's efforts had become noticeably lethargic by then, but she made up for it by exposing a little extra skin. It was well received.

I sent Horatio and Cartwright up to install the piston rings, but the lack of a Haitian Zombie was sorely felt. Particularly by the small band of Klansmen who came by to lynch him. One might have thought that the ferocious brawl that ensued—faux pirates vs. hooded spooks vs. drunken railwaymen—would put a damper on trade, but it was quite the reverse. They fought in the pasture just below the ship and I began making book on the outcome.

When the lip-biting librarian showed up with a date and another couple, I turned the bookmaking operation over to Albertson. His grasp of the mathematics involved was tenuous, but I suspected his demeanor would discourage disputes.

My guests expressed interest in having their fortunes read, so I took them inside. As soon as her beau disappeared into Mattie's cabin, I smuggled my game girl up to the crow's nest.

III

Lucy had a spacious nest—as most of her profession do—offering plenty of room for maneuvering my way into that of this frisky librarian. I tried situating her on the little bench there, but she squirmed out of my grasp and wound up sitting in my lap. Which worked out fine, as she was quite the expert little necker. While her tongue took soundings of my interior, and her hands slid about from my head to my torso, her little bottom undulated between my legs. She made no objection when I unbuttoned her blouse. I discovered the shapely, if modest, twins conveniently without further encumbrance, and promptly put my hands to work. Soon, however, she removed her mouth from mine and pulled my head to her chest. I was happy to oblige. While holding her nipples' rapt attention with my tongue, I moved a free hand up under her skirt. She sighed in apparent approval. But her thighs held firm.

"I should tell you... I've never..."

Given her frolicsome behavior during our encounter at the library—and the fact she'd come bereft of undergarments—I found this rather difficult to believe. But I withheld comment. If she wished to pretend virginity, I was perfectly happy to play along.

"Oh, don't worry. It's just a matter of preparation."

"Preparation?"

"Moistening things up...."

She relaxed her thighs enough for me to get a hand up there, and I ran a finger between the parallel shores until I found the islet I was looking for. My efforts seemed to be having the desired effect, but suddenly she pulled my hand away.

"That I can do myself."

"Well, this you can't...."

I flipped her onto the bench and knelt down between her legs.

"*No!* Nothing... exotic." She pulled me up from the floor and began unbuttoning my trousers.

Then she stopped abruptly. "There is one thing.... I mean, what are your intentions? *After* tonight?"

Her question struck me as ill-timed. "Well..."

"Because I should tell you, I've no intention of going off with you in your airship."

"No?"

"No. And I don't think you'd be willing to settle here.... That is a wedding ring, isn't it?"

I was beginning to catch her drift. "Yes. Yes, it is."

"And is she still... with us?"

"I'm on a mission now to save her from the evil pirate Lafitte."

"Good. I just wanted to make sure you weren't looking for a commitment.... OK then, let's get on with it...."

Well, after that protracted preamble, during which the fingers that had been unbuttoning my trousers remained in position throughout, even pressing against the demonstration of my ardor each time she wished to add emphasis to some syllable, I found myself perched precariously on the very edge of emancipation. I wasn't inside ten seconds before things came to a head.

"You mean... that's it?"

"Sorry. An unfortunate trait of mine.... That's why I usually spend some time on the exotic.... So no one's disappointed."

Her expression had become a good deal chillier, and her resemblance to my Latin teacher categorical.

Though out of diplomacy I didn't tell her so, I was as disappointed as she was. I'd been curious as to how she'd respond to my ministrations. Would she recite authors, by year of birth and nationality? List catalogue subject headings? Their numeric equivalent in the Dewey decimal system? I'd hoped for something along those lines, because if she stuck to lip-biting, the thing would have been a bloody pulp by the time we descended.

Oh, in case you're wondering, she *was* a virgin, after all.

"Diane? Are you up there?"

"Damnation! It's John!"

"Your beau the jealous type, is he?"

"He's not my beau. He's my brother. And he *is* rather protective."

Moments after we stepped off the ladder I found out just how protective.

"I was just giving your little sis a look at the crow's nest," I told him.

The parrot, which had apparently been spying on us, flew down and landed on the girl's shoulder.

"*Nothing exotic,*" he mimicked. "*OK, let's get on with it....*" He had her intonation down pat.

At first, her brother didn't seem to notice me. His

eyes moved directly from the bird to a patch of dampness gracing the lap of his kinswoman's skirt. When he did turn his attention to me, he wordlessly shared his feelings.

I awoke to the sun cresting the horizon. Members of the crew lay about me in various attitudes of repose. From the looks of things, I surmised they'd issued themselves a sizable ration of rum.

I went out to relieve myself and found the pasture a veritable trash heap of celebratory excess. Hats, shirts, shoes, candy wrappers, perforated sheets, Cracker Jack boxes, and more than a few bodies littered the hillside. I even came across a couple abandoned prizes.

By then, Horatio and Mattie were up and about. While she went off to fix breakfast, I queried her companion.

"Did you get the piston rings on OK?"

"Oh, yes. Everything is ready."

"Good. I wonder what sort of profit we made?"

"Profit? Well, the gate was good. Even after paying off your railwayman, there was a few hundred left. But about two o'clock, when most everyone else had gone home, a big barouche arrived—with some very friendly ladies on board...."

"Oh.... Just how friendly?"

"Friendly enough. They went home with most of the profits."

"Couldn't you have stopped them?"

"Well, this was after the men found the rum, and they seemed to like the arrangement. But don't be too sad. I doubt it would have been enough to bid on your wife in St. Pierre."

"I'm told the auction house prefers payment in fine

liquor. I was hoping for some capital to invest in it."

"Then I suppose you'll need to take on some rum-runners."

"I'd rather not. They seem as well armed as we are. And their liquor is only sometimes fine. I was thinking we might raid a steamship. The boats of the French Line come pretty well stocked."

"Wouldn't that be a little *too* ironic? You raiding a French steamship to make right the raiding of a French steamship? I think you might tax the goodwill of your readers."

One doesn't expect a critique of this sort from the first mate of a privateer, especially as I had no idea at the time I'd be committing these reminiscences to paper. But his point was well taken. Besides, finding a liner of a particular flag at sea might prove problematic.

A messenger arrived by bicycle a little later with a response to my wire in which I asked Cousin Emmie how to return to the normal world:

Whyever would you want to?

It was signed neither by Emmie nor by one of her pen names, but by Walt Whitman. How'd the old pond snipe manage to get back to Brooklyn?

That was a question I suspect had no answer. Nonetheless, the news of his presence led me to wonder if this fictional world was not Emmie's alone.

"Hey, where's my cooch show!" the messenger broke in.

"I'm afraid the coocher is indisposed. She had a long night. How about a shot of rum?"

"For climbing that damn hill? Make it a pint."

He drank half of it before beginning his descent. I was happy for this reminder that fictional Prohibition worked about as well as the real one because it brought to mind F. Scott Fitzgerald.

I happened to have met the renowned author and souse at a hotel bar in Le Havre. He'd just arrived from New York, while we were waiting to board the S.S. *Paris*. He talked to me at some length about a novel he was working on. It centered on a shady character of great wealth who held lavish parties featuring huge quantities of expensive liquor. He was particularly pleased with the name of the town on Long Island where the great man lived. He'd christened it West Egg.

Scott, as he insisted I call him, told me he hadn't really gotten to writing the thing. But I wondered if his preliminary notes might not be enough to influence the world we currently inhabited. I consulted the atlas, and sure enough, there on the north shore of Long Island someone had penciled in West Egg. Just across the bay from where East Egg had been deposited. Laid there, no doubt, by my eccentric cousin.

The bay on which West Egg sat was almost exactly where Congdon's parched estate lay, back in the land of nonfiction. Monkey wrench in hand, I roused the crew. As soon as we were airborne, I gave the men a stirring oratory, reminding them of our mission to make safe American womanhood. This netted me a field of dubious looks. So I told them a good haul of liquor was anticipated. Cheers all around. But now came the negotiating.

We settled on an even split: for every case of hooch put toward saving American womanhood, one would be set aside for the crew. I insisted, however, on one proviso: I was to choose who got which case. They readily acceded. Only the rare Navy gob could interpret a foreign label, and fewer still cared what they poured down their gullet so long as it got the job done.

We arrived about noon. The servants were still cleaning up after the prior night's revelry. But just as I'd hoped, the estate was otherwise unguarded. The crew—still in pirate costume from their performance back in Port Jervis—herded the startled staff into the kitchen and swiftly set up a bucket brigade from the house's cavernous cellars to *Lucy*'s hold. Purloining liquor was the one thing they excelled at.

"Just how much can the ship carry?" I asked Horatio.

"Oh, liquor? All she can get! Never known *Lucy* to turn down a drink."

He was right about that. She was a sort of inverse cornucopia. I counted one hundred thirty-seven cases of champagne; an almost equal number of fine Scotch; three dozen each of cognac, schnapps, and first-rate gin; miscellaneous cases of every liqueur you can imagine; and a near-inexhaustible supply of French and Italian wines. The crew's allocation consisted of vast quantities of rum, vodka, and the lesser gins and whiskeys; multiple casks of port and sherry; and ninety-three kegs of beer. I spoke briefly with the butler, and he swore this was barely a three-week supply. Fictional folk certainly know how to throw a party.

We were just finishing up when Woese asked to speak to me.

"I changed my mind. I think I'll take my chances here, if it's all the same to you."

"I see. But eventually we'll be headed home. I mean, the right home. Don't you want to see your people again?"

"Well, sure, I guess. But I've been thinking. Maybe

that other me in New York can get *me* a job in radio. How could I afford to pass up a chance like that?"

I had no answer. I sent him off with my blessings and a bottle of good Scotch with which to soften up his fictitious self. Then we set off.

The afternoon sun burned bright—a lucky happenstance since the crew had drunk themselves into a collective stupor within minutes of boarding. I set course for the northeast and we made excellent time. Until, that is, we hit a patch of rain that evening over New Brunswick. The only ones sober enough to man the oars were myself, Cartwright, the two women, and Horatio. I left him on the bridge and joined the other three in the oar room. The females sat down together, but I had Mattie move to the opposite side with Cartwright. I was worried an imbalance of strength would have us going in a circle. And my concern was warranted. Dottie was built like a teamster, and Mattie was no cream puff herself.

About eleven, much earlier than I expected, Horatio called on the voice tube to say he had spotted the isles of St. Pierre and Miquelon. Or, as he put it, *probably* had.

CHAPTER 11.

A THING WORTH DOING

IS WORTH DOING WELL

In fact, we were not over St. Pierre and Miquelon, but rather over the Îles de la Madeleine, 300 miles to the west. The prevailing wind had died and Horatio had failed to compensate. I admonished him. But he pointed to the difficulty of navigating on a starless night.

"And that map, it ain't no good."

"What do you mean? All you needed to do was keep to the east coast of Nova Scotia, then continue on that course." I showed him on the atlas. He just shook his head. I'd learned earlier he held a deep-seated distrust of maps.

"Yes, on the map! But Nova Scotia wasn't there! I figured we'd gone by it."

I looked back down at the atlas and noticed a small notation made in pencil beside the province in question: *See page 59.* Turning to that page, I found the islands of the Southwest Pacific, and penciled in next to New Caledonia: *aka Nova Scotia.* Apparently, Cousin Emmie felt a need to economize on islands. I turned back to confirm St. Pierre was where it should be and was relieved to see no emendations. There was, however, a notation in the same hand beside Prince Edward Island: *Mythical.*

I corrected course, then—with a few well-placed kicks to the head—assembled a squad to man the oars. We made poor time, no more than twenty-five knots. But that was just as well. We'd arrive at dawn the day before the auction. Plenty of time to ascertain if Sesbania numbered among the goods destined for the block.

Suddenly, we heard a loud splat, like a hand slapping water. Then two more. *Lucy* began to shake uncontrollably.

"That's not the rings again, is it?" I asked Horatio.

"No. Something much worse.... Look!"

I followed his nod to the window. There, in the weak glow of our lamps, I could see the tentacle of a sea creature. Its suckers had made fast to the ship.

"*To the boats!*" the parrot squawked. "*Women and parrots first!*"

I threw an empty rum bottle at him, but he just flew to another roost. "*Ah, ishkabibble!*"

There was another splat....

"How is this even possible?" I asked Horatio. "We're flying at eight hundred feet."

"Yes, but so is *he*."

"What sort of sea monster sails in the sky?"

"The worst kind: Captain Bonnet, the mad pirate of Barbados."

Splat!

"Tell me, when you say mad, are you referring to the condition of his mind? Or his general disposition?"

"The first, always. The second, only when things don't go his way."

"Is he after liquor?"

"Who isn't? But mostly Captain Bonnet hunts just two things...." *Splat!* "The first is men."

"To join his crew?"

"To marry his daughters."

Splat!

"How many daughters could he have?"

"Oh, dozens. And he keeps making more."

"His poor wife…"

Splat!

"*Wives*. He's Mormon."

"What's the second thing he hunts?"

"Books. Old books. The older the better." *Splat!* "Very strange fellow."

By then *Lucy* had been thoroughly engulfed in tentacles and we were being pulled upward.

"I'm going up to the crow's nest to see what I can make out," I told him. "Better wake up the rest of the crew…. At least those still among the living."

Halfway up, my path was blocked by someone descending. I deferred to his bulk and met him at the foot of the ladder. He was a queer-looking bird, dressed in full eighteenth-century pirate regalia, with long gray hair flowing out from under a tricorne hat. Odder still, his features bore a striking resemblance to those of Rutledge, the bond trader I'd left back in New York. He looked at me perplexed, as I am sure I did him.

"Ah, Captain Bonnet, I presume. I am Captain Van Slyke."

"Are you now?" He gave my mustache a little tug in lieu of a handshake.

"May I ask the reason for this effrontery?"

"I am Bonnet, *the mad pirate*. That's all the reason I need. Assemble your men at once for boarding. I mean to take your crew, Captain."

"And if I refuse to submit and choose to fight?"

He was armed with nothing more than a small dagger (which I later learned was used solely for opening correspondence), so I thought I could afford to be aggressive.

"I'll appeal to your men directly. I've thirty-odd daughters looking for mates, all beauties and all untouched by the hands of men. Each comes with a dowry of one thousand pieces of eight, plus a beginner's library consisting of the complete works of Shakespeare, Pope's editions of Homer, North's Plutarch, Florio's *Decameron*, and selections from Ovid, Virgil, and Martial in the original Latin with handy translations on facing pages.... So, you see, it won't be me you'll be needing to fight."

He seemed to have a keen knowledge of my crew's character—though not their reading habits.

"And if I give you the men, will you allow me and my first mate, both already betrothed, to go on our way?"

"Fair enough." He shook my hand. "But I insist you come aboard and join me for the evening feast."

I asked if the invitation extended to Horatio and our two women, and he affirmed that it did. But all three were too wary to accept.

"If you take my advice, you'll stay with *Lucy*," Mattie told me.

"What can it hurt? We won't be able to get under way until sunrise anyway."

Looking back, it would have been wise to heed her counsel. But after days of Spartan fare, a feast sounded too tempting to pass up. Especially one attended by a comely brood of females numbering in the dozens. Besides, once the sun rose, Horatio and I could easily make our way to St. Pierre without the men.

As expected, the crew saw much to admire in Bonnet's offer. There was, however, one bone of contention. Being a devout Mormon, the captain ran a dry ship. No doubt this accounted for his trouble in finding sons-in-law. Eventually, he and the men arrived at a compromise: their liquor would be held in escrow until they had been wedded and deposited with their wives on terra firma. Then they could do as their consciences directed—and they certainly couldn't hope for greater latitude than that.

Once we'd boarded, Bonnet took me to his cabin. Like the rest of the ship, it was decorated in high baroque fashion, and few surfaces left free of lavish embellishment and gilded ornamentation. The gratuitous excess of the style must have afforded craftsmen of the time an excellent opportunity to line their pockets.

No sooner had we sat down than he began waxing on about the merits of Mormonism.

"Why, a man of your abilities could easily support five or six wives."

"I thought Mormons had given up on polygamy."

"You've obviously never been to southern Utah!"

I gladly conceded his point, and he took that as a cue to resume his tribute to his idyllic family life. Being an American, I am well used to being proselytized by delusionals of the sundry churches and sects which pepper our great nation. But he was the first to present a truly sound spiritual argument. He did this by means of his daughters.

"Ah, here are Clotho, Lachesis, and Atropos." A statuesque blonde, a fetching brunette, and a raven-haired splendor had entered the room, each bearing a tray of sweetmeats and wearing a robe in the classical Greek style. "It's they who constructed those diabolical tentacles. From the lining of cows' intestines, sewn together with immaculate stitching. Steam-powered, naturally."

I assumed he meant the tentacles, but the three girls

looked equally capable of raising one's temperature—*if* they were in the mood. At the moment, that seemed not to be the case. The first two contented themselves with displays of annoyance at his awkward paean. The ebon-tressed Atropos, however, looked downright incensed.

"Of course, I'd prefer they go as a set," her father continued.

She cut him off with an audible sneer. "No one sets a course for us!" she hissed, then quickly led her sisters out of the room.

"Lovely girls, the Fates," he said. "But there's no getting around the fact they *can* be a little headstrong. Even, at times, cruel."

"Yes, so I've heard."

"I suppose I should've expected they'd acquired a reputation. I'm hoping I can find someone looking for a challenge." He gave a small shake of his head. "So, how long have you been running rum?"

"Oh, that's mere cover. I've no real interest in the stuff." I didn't want to appear the blasphemer. "I'm on a mission to recover some womenfolk who were abducted by pirates from an ocean liner, the S.S. *Paris*. Perhaps you heard of the incident?"

"Not 'til now. You don't think I had anything to do with it, do you?"

"No, I can see your problem lies in the other direction. I believe the fiendish Lafitte was behind it. And that he plans to auction his wares on Thursday. Or at least the lot that consists of my wife."

"Your wife? Taken by Lafitte? Mightn't it be wise then to have one or two in reserve?"

"Well, there's no denying there'd be obvious advantages...."

"Dinner is served, Father." It was another inviting maiden. She'd opened the door without making a sound.

"All right, Irene. We'll be along in a moment." She gave us the most serene smile I've ever seen, then quietly stepped out again. "One of the Horae," he told me. "Very useful if you forget to wind your chronometer."

"Yes, I'm sure. Well, getting back to my story: I've been commissioned by the president...."

"What president?"

"American. You see, I'm a retired naval officer...."

"Are you now? So's my son-in-law, Smedley. Went to Annapolis."

"What a remarkable coincidence. So did I."

"Good. Then I'll let him talk to you about terms...."

"Terms?"

He didn't answer. He was already up and holding the door for me. "Come along, feast first. Negotiatin' after."

He led me to a large dining room, one even more extravagantly decorated than his office. The ceiling and walls were covered in frescoes, scenes of fleshy women falling out of their modest attire and attended to by a variety of fauns, satyrs, and buccaneers. I couldn't help but wonder what Brigham Young would have made of it.

Once we'd sat down, he introduced me to several of his wives. They all had difficult foreign names, like Mnemosyne, and Eurynome. The Fates sat at the table with us, as did their far more affable sisters, the Graces. And the Horae, and some—but not all nine—of the Muses. Plus the husbands of those who were married, including the fellow Smedley. His mother-in-law, Eurynome, was first to comment on the similarity of our looks. Personally, I couldn't see it. But it did explain why Bonnet had tugged my mustache: Smedley was clean-shaven.

The feast opened with squid cooked in its own ink, the younger daughters doing the serving—dryads, mostly, though a few of them appeared to be oceanids who hadn't had time to towel off. The second course was goat in a jerk sauce. Then came a salad, and then oranges—mine brought by a playful naiad, who peeled it for me with far more suggestiveness than you might imagine possible.

Without wine, the meal lacked a certain conviviality. The only conversation I took part in was with the woman seated to my right. She was quite friendly, and seemed genuinely interested in my story—a very pleasant girl. However, her attentions fell well short of flirting. And, much to my annoyance, she spent an equal amount of time with the fellow on her right.

Happily, the sea of feminine forms gliding about the table provided ample distraction. So damp were the oceanids, their robes had become all but transparent. I was still ogling them over my dessert when Smedley rose and beckoned me out. Just in time, he told me. Polyhymnia was about to treat the gathering to a solemn canticle.

II

He took me to his own cabin, and there poured us some refreshment from a silver statuette.

"Brandy," he said. "There's some very good Scotch in that lamp, if you'd prefer."

"No, brandy's fine."

"The old man said you were at Annapolis. What year?"

"Class of '15. You?"

He laughed. "No good, old sport. I was class of '15. And I don't think I could have missed meeting you."

I laughed along with him. Better he think me a liar than have to explain that his class—and, in fact, his very being—was mere fiction.

"Don't worry. The secret's ours. The old man thinks you might be good for three or four of the sisters-in-law."

"How many wives have you?"

"Just the one, Euphrosyne. You've probably heard of her—one of the Graces. You were seated next to her at dinner."

"Oh, yes. Lovely girl. I suppose she'd object if you were to take another."

"Her? Oh, no. She's a joy. Never complains about anything. No, I'm just considering my options."

"Yes, they're nothing if not attractive...."

"Well, for the most part. Of course, you haven't seen Gluttony. And if you think the Fates are disagreeable, you should meet Wrath and Pride—and Envy and Avarice aren't much better. But that's getting around to my point. You see, Bonnet is no fool. He knows no one in their right mind will take on a Mortal Sin without due compensation. Why, he's offered as much as five thousand pounds sterling to the man who will take Wrath off his hands. *And* to throw in a pair of naiads as well—you can imagine how frisky they are."

"If their efforts in the bedroom are anything like those of the one who peeled my orange, I certainly can imagine. But your inventory of Sins seems to have left out Lust. Is she by any chance...?"

"Not currently available, I'm afraid. She's a problem of a different sort. No trouble finding her a mate, of course. But she goes through them at the most torrid pace. Heart attacks, usually. She's living in Fresno, California, right now with husband number four—or is it five? She'll be back here within a few months. No, there's no two ways about it: a Mortal Sin is a handful."

"What about the Virtues?"

"The Virtues? Oh, they're still all available—and at market price."

"Market price?"

"Well, with Faith and Fortitude you get the standard thousand pieces of eight."

"Plus the beginner's library?"

"Oh, that goes with all of them. With Charity and Hope, we could go double that—an acknowledgment that goodness can be grating. Justice and Prudence—very tiresome—say... five thousand each?"

"Sounds not unreasonable. But who's that leave?"

"Temperance. She's another problem child. See, the old man views her as a genuine Virtue, but not many others are likely to see eye to eye with him."

"Perhaps another Mormon?"

"Ideally. Or a Mohammedan, but we don't encounter many of either."

"One thing puzzles me. Where's the money come from? I mean, how's Bonnet finance all this without involving himself in the rum trade?"

"What makes you think he's not involved in it?"

"Well, he runs a dry ship."

"Oh, yes. He's adamant on that. But he doesn't feel dealing in the stuff contradicts his convictions—provided there's no imbibing of it in his presence. Like most theologies, when it comes to business, Mormonism is infinitely pliable. All the better hotels in New York buy from dear Father. Even owns a string of bars in the pirate ports."

"Not the ones featuring alarmed pelicans?"

"Yes, quite a popular theme."

"Though not, perhaps, with the birds."

"No, I suppose not."

It was then that the ugly truth hit me. "Bonnet brought me aboard so he could steal my stores without my stopping him."

"Yes, I'm afraid he did. From what I hear, they were quite extensive—all choice stuff."

"It is. And I need it desperately to get my wife back from the evil Lafitte. She's to be auctioned on Thursday. Can't you, as a fellow Annapolis man, have a word with him?"

"I wouldn't try playing that card if I were you. And it's for an auction that Bonnet wants your liquor."

"What? Bidding on another wife?"

"No, no. We arrive Saturday. That's when antiquities are auctioned. He's heard there's an early edition of something by Shakespeare. Bonnet collects that sort of thing."

"Run pretty dear, do they?"

"Oh, yes. But I don't think we'll be needing your entire stock. So I suppose we might come to some arrangement...."

Negotiations ran nearly until dawn. I wound up taking a mixed set. I figured Wrath and Avarice could actually come in handy, and what harm could come from Faith, Hope, and Fortitude? Then I impulsively snapped up Erato at first mention of her name—though as soon as we'd shaken on the deal, he confessed the cognomen was something of a misnomer.

"It is lively stuff, but I'm afraid all she wants to do is recite it...."

As dowry, he offered the return of seventy-four cases of champagne, sixty-nine of fine Scotch, and two dozen of the good gin.

"I don't suppose you could throw in some of the liqueurs?"

"Well, can you take on Melpomene as well?"

"Who's she?"

"You know, another Muse. Sings. Wonderful voice."

The moment I agreed, he admitted dramatic tragedy was her principal purview. In my defense, I would simply note that one doesn't expect to need a copy of *Bullfinch's Mythology* when entering negotiations with pirates.

On the way out of his cabin, he handed me a wad of cotton.

"Stuff it in your ears. We've got to pass by the Limnads. They're usually carrying on this time of day."

"Who are they?"

"Nymphs of lakes, marshes, and swamps. Have a penchant for giving out false calls of distress and luring men to their doom. Otherwise, they're lovely girls."

We gathered up my harem and Bonnet himself performed a quick ceremony. The brides were all attractive, each in her own way, but of varying complexions and features. So much so, I found it difficult to believe they shared a father. Nevertheless, I deemed it unwise to inquire. It's a dangerous business probing the fidelity of another man's wife—especially when the cuckold in question is a mad pirate.

My new wives evinced little interest in the ritual. Or in me, for that matter. But they seemed downright enthusiastic about leaving their father's custody. All except the girl on my far right. She had trouble just staying awake.

They arrived aboard *Lucy* with a procession of servants bearing their vast trousseaux: wardrobes, furnish-
ings, and an endless train of miscellaneous finery. As
soon as they'd unloaded, I sent the menials back. I'd
accepted a consignment of seven wives, not a small army
of retainers. My brides protested, of course. But I told
them to return to their father if they were unhappy with
the arrangement. Not one of them did. Most fathers are
prone to play the tyrant now and again, but *pirate* fathers—particularly *mad* pirate fathers—must be something else altogether. The girls did, however, take a firm
stand on Percival. He was a steamfitter they'd brought
along, wisely anticipating the inadequacy of *Lucy's*
plumbing.

To my surprise, Albertson returned as well. To be
with his Dottie, he said. I suspect the real reason was that
he'd been rejected by all Bonnet's daughters. But Dottie
believed him, and that was all that mattered.

By then the sun had risen, and with the wind at our
backs, we were making excellent time. It would still take
several hours to reach St. Pierre, so I went into my cabin
for a nap—alone. With seven young wives, you might
think that odd. But I hadn't as yet committed to memory
just who was who. I thought Fortitude might be game—or
at least could be counted on not to flee—but what if I
propositioned Wrath by mistake?

The cabin was dark and it wasn't until I was getting
into bed that I noticed it was already occupied. She was
sound asleep, facing away. Her robe was half off and her
long black hair loose about her. I slid in beside her and
she made no objections. I began with petting and fondling and moans of delight soon followed. She turned
toward me. Sleepy almond eyes, and naturally puckered

lips, as if ever ready for a kiss. I'd lay odds, her father was not Bonnet but some pirate plying the South China Sea.

"Would you mind giving me a massage?" She had the most sultry, languid voice I've ever heard.

She turned on her stomach and I began kneading her shoulders. She moaned some more, but by the time I worked down to her flawless fanny, I could hear snoring. I turned her over and kissed her awake.

"I'm afraid I've forgotten your name."

"I'm... Fortitude...." Her eyes were mere slits.

I went to work below deck and the moans came fast and furious. Then, suddenly, they stopped.... A moment later she was once more snoring. I didn't have the energy to wake her up again, so I just snuggled up beside her and fell asleep. In my dreams, at least, she was a first-rate performer.

On rising from bed several hours later, I watched her for a few moments. Sleep became her. Then the truth dawned on me: I'd been sold a bill of goods. This wasn't Fortitude, this was her opposite number, Sloth. The same girl who'd slept through the wedding.

I found the other girls up on the oar deck, squabbling violently. I need hardly tell you, they weren't at all pleased with the accommodations. They had decided to subdivide the space with curtains and were now negotiating borders. Eventually, I was able to calm them enough to take a roll.

Just as I suspected, I'd been had. Not only had Fortitude been supplanted by Sloth, but Faith and Hope had been swapped out for Pride and Envy. I had five of the seven Mortal Sins, and not a single Virtue!

Not helping matters, Melpomene sat in a corner throughout, singing lamentations. She did, indeed, have a lovely voice. But I've a limited appetite for elegies, dirges, and threnodies. Especially on an empty stomach.

"We've arrived at St. Pierre," Horatio announced through the voice tube.

Happy for the interruption, I joined him in the control room. This time, he had guessed correctly.

I wasn't sure if fictional marriage could be judged as bigamy, but I did feel some trepidation about introducing Sesbania into the mix as number eight. She wasn't the jealous type, generally. But she firmly believed all even numbers to be unlucky.

III

After a brief repast, Albertson and I were lowered to the surface. I teased him about his romantic gesture—turning down Bonnet's offer of gold and returning to Dottie. Rather than becoming angry, he appeared embarrassed. So completely had love softened him, he was actually solicitous about Sesbania. In his way.

"Whattaya think she'll fetch at auction?"

"I'm afraid the bidding's likely to go fairly high. Her finer points will be in full view, but not her impetuous temperament."

"A hellion, is she?"

"I wouldn't call her that. She works more subtly."

"Ya mean... cunnin'?"

"Yes, that's her."

"Ain't love strange?"

It certainly was. It had made a philosopher out of the coarsest gob in the Navy.

We entered the Sans Souci Auction House—owned and operated by Lafitte Bros., Inc.—and I asked to preview the next day's lots. There was a good bit of finery—a few gowns and dresses, but menswear mostly—and yard upon yard of colorful silk on the bolt. It seemed to be the pirate's textile of choice, arising from the lack of under-garments, I assume.

Also displayed were various pieces of jewelry. I asked if they had wedding rings and a clerk showed me an entire case—but he stubbornly refused to create a seven-piece lot for my pleasure.

"What about women?"

"No combining lots of *any* wares!"

"But you do have some on the docket for tomor-row?"

"Just one tomorrow. Wanna see her?"

"Yes, if it wouldn't be an inconvenience."

"Won't be no inconvenience for me. But remember, no touchin'! You want to see her teeth, she'll open her mouth for you."

"Very accommodating."

He led us upstairs to a little sitting room which was divided in two by a wall of steel bars. Then he rang a little gong. Sesbania emerged from some inner sanctum. She appeared uncharacteristically cowed, wearing a simple frock, and in bare feet. I was moved. But I withheld any signs of recognition. Given the frequency with which doppelgangers had been dropping in on me, I didn't want to give myself away before being sure.

She, however, was not so restrained. On seeing me, she rushed the barrier.

"Oh, Pluribus! I knew you'd come!"

She reached through the bars and hugged me as she'd never hugged me before.

"None of that!" the auction clerk said.

She was crying now.

"Look, can't you leave us alone for just a minute?" I asked.

"No! ...Want her to drop the togs?"

"You cur!" I grabbed the insolent blackguard by the collar. "How dare you speak of her like that?"

He pulled a blackjack from his belt and was about to let me have it when Albertson did likewise to him.

I searched him in vain for keys. Albertson had better luck with his wallet, but wasn't sure what to make of the French currency.

"Quick!" Sesbania implored me. "The others will be back soon. When they see what you've done... Oh, leave now, while you have the chance!"

"Never!" Her selfless spirit steeled my resolve—right up to the very moment heavily shod feet began ascending the stairs. "Well, all right.... But rest assured, I'll be back for you!"

Our parting kiss was like no other I'd ever experienced. Albertson opened a window and I followed him out onto the roof of a porch, and from there, to the street below. As we merged into the crowd, he reached over and patted my shoulder. There were tears running down his cheeks. I wasn't sure I didn't prefer the old Albertson.

On reaching the ship, I went immediately to the hold to check on the girls' dowries. Unlike the girls themselves, I *had* confirmed the authenticity of the liquor—but only by label. Now I wanted to be sure.

I opened a bottle of the Moët & Chandon. It uncorked with a reassuring pop, but on tasting I found it had been replaced by carbonated cider! And the Monopole by ginger ale. Similarly, the gin was just lime-flavored water. And the so-called Scotch only cheap rum.

For the moment, however, I was happy to have it. I'd just taken a third long swig of the stuff when someone spun me around from behind.

"What's she got that I haven't got!"

It was one of my harem. I remembered her from the ceremony, as she was the only one who'd scrutinized my appearance. On closer inspection, she looked more ordinary than I remembered—bobbed brunette hair, small eyes, thin lips, and a figure that came very near to squat. But there lurked a curious nervous energy about her, as if she were just waiting for something, or someone, to set her off. For the moment, however, her name escaped me.

"What's who got?"

"Sloth! That layabout—how could you have chosen her?"

Envy, apparently.

"I didn't choose her...."

"Well, I'll make you forget all about her. And the others!"

When first we'd met, she'd been barely civil. I saw a different side of her now. She had me unclothed and supine within seconds, and soon was doing unto me as I'd so frequently done to others. In no time, she had me on the brink—then stopped. Her tongue skittered about my belly, and now her bare breasts were caressing that which her lips had so recently attended. But no sooner had she returned me to the precipice than she repositioned herself once more and was soon sitting astride my chest.

"Now, how would you like a taste of a *real* woman?"

She precluded any sort of verbal reply by lifting my head and fastening my mouth to what we in the Navy refer to as a lady's aphrodisiacal fore hatch. But reply I did.

As her excitement grew, she began a sort of choleric chant, sometimes lapsing into Latin, more often Greek. I couldn't make much of it out, but the gist seemed to be an enumeration of her sisters' faults. And they being Mortal Sins, the list was a long one.

Eventually, she sidled back down and straddled me. I didn't last long, as usual, but rather than minding, she took it as confirmation of her sexual supremacy.

"Now, tell me, how did Sloth compare to that?"

"No contest, really. You're in a class by yourself."

She smiled contentedly. I knew how to play to an audience.

Bonnet had said they were all virgins, and there was some evidence that she had been. But I couldn't imagine where she'd learned her technique. I asked her about it and she told me her father's literary tastes ran far and wide.

"The French novels are the best. And, when we were younger, I shared a bed with Lust...."

"Ah, say no more."

I wouldn't have minded lingering on our uncomfortable bed a little longer. But her mind could not easily be stilled, and soon her thoughts gravitated to her sisters.

"I'll bet they're divvying up all the best linens without me. Avarice, that bitch, is always going through my things. Then there's those damn Muses! Father always favored them.... *And* the Graces... Damn little prisses! Most insipid of all were the Virtues—made me want to vomit! All we heard as children was, 'Why can't you girls be like your sisters?' And meanwhile, the Fates got away with murder...."

By now she had re-robed, and soon hurried off to defend her property rights.

Once I'd dressed, I followed her out. We found the entire ship's company on the former oar deck, riveted by Albertson's teary-eyed account of Sesbania's predicament and my all-too-brief reunion with her. Mattie and Dottie were likewise wiping away tears, while Melpomene wailed like a widow who's discovered she married her own son. The others merely listened with interest. All except Sloth, of course. She was sound asleep, her head in Erato's lap.

Needless to say, Envy found the scene thoroughly amusing. She giggled to herself—but curiously, said nothing. The parrot, unfortunately, was not so discreet.

"*Now, how would you like a taste of a real woman?*"

After tossing a handy fork in his direction, I turned my most desolate face to the others.

"I'm afraid things are even worse than I realized," I told them. "It seems Captain Bonnet stuck me with inferior goods."

"What!" It was Pride.

"Sorry. I wasn't being clear. I meant the liquor. I needed it to bid on Sesbania. Your father substituted ginger ale for Monopole."

"So what will you do?" asked Horatio.

"I don't know. If anyone has any suggestions, I'll be in my cabin. For now, we'll just maintain our position."

I went in and poured myself a tall brandy—then peered out the porthole at the setting sun. Sesbania never allowed a sunset to transpire without taking note, always finding something pleasing in it. I was becoming teary-eyed myself.

"I've a proposition." Avarice had snuck up beside me without my hearing.

She stood as tall as I did and I could feel her warm breath on my face. Hers was framed by a fetching mop of bobbed blonde hair—the outer layer the color of straw, but darker underneath, as if bleached by the sun. It curled inward just an inch or two below her ears, and had a beguiling way of shifting about whenever she turned her head. At the moment, however, it lay still.

While her intense hazel eyes held me prisoner in their gaze, a teasing tongue ran across her ruby lips. "That is, *if* you're interested."

"I'm flattered," I told her. "But I'm not sure I could just now."

"*No, you ass!* I'm not that slut, Envy. And you don't need to fake any tears for me."

"You cut me to the quick...."

"Oh, give it a rest, you hypocrite! Look, there's only one thing I want: *money*. And I have a plan that will satisfy us both—assuming you really do want what's-her-name back."

"Sesbania. She's named for a flowering vine. And I very much would like her back."

"Well, I haven't worked out all the details, but here's the nub of it: we break her out by working from the inside."

"How do we do that?"

"Convince the other girls to allow themselves to be put on the block. Then when they're taken to wherever they keep their captives, they break out."

"That could be far more difficult than you think. Lafitte's men are ruthless pirates. Cutthroats."

"Oh, for Christ's sake! We're talking Deadly Sins

here! You've never seen Wrath in action. And, it so happens, her Aunt Flo is visiting—what little she has in the way of restraint flies out the window when the cramps arrive. Pride I can talk into anything. All child psychology with her. And Envy. I've been playing her like a violin since we left the cradle. Sloth's a lost cause, of course. And I doubt those whining Muses will be much use in a fight. By the way, did you know the one calling herself Erato is actually Clio?"

"Clio? What's her domain?"

"History, mostly, and heroic exploits. But in her case the switch wasn't Father's doing. He preferred keeping her as his librarian. Willing to work for peanuts, the sap. But she's always envied her sisters their mellifluous voices, particularly Erato's. She's been taking lessons. They're identical twins, so Father didn't notice. But we're straying from the subject. The crux of the plan is that the girls bring them down from within."

"It's an admirable scheme, but what do you get out of it? I mean no offense, but..."

"Yes, of course there's something in it for me! I don't act out of charity."

"Did I meet her?"

"Forget Charity and listen! Father used me as his accountant. Treated me like a slave! Paid me next to nothing, and never trusted me with the cash."

"Well, to be fair, given the name..."

"*Watch it!* Anyway, once a month or so, he sent Smedley and myself to each of the Pelicans in his string to go over the accounts and collect the profits—and they are *very* profitable. Surely you noticed, you're a perfect double for Smedley—provided you shave off that hideous mustache."

I felt insulted. But all the same, it would have to go before Sesbania arrived. She abhorred facial hair, and I'd only begun growing it since her abduction.

"So we collect the profits before Smedley and your father arrive?"

"Correct. They're not expected until Saturday. We grab the loot, the girls stage their uprising, we scoop them up along with your weedy vine, and off we go!"

"Yes, sounds promising. But just out of curiosity, what prevents these managers from hiding the profits from you?"

"Well, of course they do. One can only hope to minimize it. Periodically, Father has one killed—and not pleasantly."

"I see. Just one more thing: what sort of split are you proposing for the loot?"

"Shall we say 80-20? After all, it's my plan. And you need me to convince the girls, not to mention the manager of the Pelican. And you *are* getting back—what did you call her? Poison Ivy?"

"Only in her darkest moods. Generally, it's Sesbania. How about 60-40?"

She laughed. "More worried about your split than your jilt.... Maybe I *could* get to like you.... But not that much. We'll say 75-25, and that's final."

She took pen and paper from the desk and put it all in writing, then called in Horatio and Mattie to witness our signatures. One doesn't expect Sins to be so punctilious.

CHAPTER 12.

SIN THAT'S HIDDEN IS HALF-FORGIVEN

At long last, I was on the very brink of rescuing my dear Sesbania. I'd imagined this moment many times since I began the expedition. Believe it or not, I'm something of a romantic in my reveries. I'd heroically vanquished any number of pirates, rum-runners, and Amazons to reclaim my fair girl.

At this particular moment, however, I was receiving a shave at the hand of the fair Avarice. Having finished the left side of my face, she turned my head so she could see the right side in the mirror. As she did, my left cheek drew across her right nipple. She was wearing her robe, of course, but they come pretty sheer. And beneath it— nothing. She'd been speculating on our take, and as the numbers swelled in size, so did her nipple. Not one to be left behind, my own little fellow made his thoughts known as well.

Whether her lips made the first move or my hand, I can't say for sure. But within seconds we were writhing on the floor, entwined. Well, entangled, actually. The thing about those long robes is, while it's quite easy to jettison them from a standing position, once you're recumbent, it's next to impossible. All you can do is work around them. Luckily, I knew what I was looking for and she wasn't at all hesitant about making it available.

I went at it in earnest and soon had her tallying the accrued balance on her expected share of the profits, first if invested in British gilts, then in South African mining stocks—with all interest and dividends reinvested, and thereby compounded.

Every once in a while her voice would shoot up an octave. But whether that was due to my efforts or simply satisfaction with her return, I couldn't be certain. So I kept at it, trying all sorts of little variations, and for twice as long as usual. She gave no unequivocal signs of approval. But anytime I paused, she shouted, *"More!"*—and in a tone closer to that of a plantation overseer than of an impassioned lover.

She'd just reached the year 2034, when I realized my mouth was bone dry.... "If I could just..."

"No talking!" she ordered, then locked her thighs about my head.

Under normal circumstances, I found this maneuver erotic. But these were thighs that could crack a coconut. It was once more into the breach, and pray I'd be among the survivors.... By the year 2112, my lips felt as they had after my debut performance playing the Sousaphone in the school band.

Then, suddenly, the iron thighs relaxed. "Get up! We've no more time for love-making," she announced.

I noticed she was still holding the razor, so I made no protest. Besides, my mouth was too dry to make a response of any kind.

"Maybe I'll give you another chance later." She straightened her gown and checked herself in the mirror. Then it was back to business. "I've already briefed Wrath, Envy, and Clio. They're all agreeable. Melpomene I thought we could bring to the Pelican and use to distract the manager while I pocket the till. She's actually a fairly decent chanteuse, with a nice repertoire of songs on unrequited love. Though not much in the looks department. Pride, as usual, refuses to follow a plan not her own. She says she'll come along, but only if she can be part of the floor show. Her voice is no great shakes, but I think we can get her to drop the robe—that should prove something of a diversion."

Since Horatio would be taking Clio and the two Sins to the auction house, Albertson would be left in command of the ship. But I thought it unlikely he'd abandon us. Especially since he reconfirmed his incompetence as we were leaving by pointing at the compass and telling me the chronometer had stopped.

When we neared our destination, Avarice handed Horatio a horsewhip to use as a prop. (Why she had such a device amidst her trousseau was a question I thought best left unasked.) He cracked it over the heads of his three captives, and they acted suitably cowed. Wrath whimpered convincingly, and then Envy did her one better by wailing uncontrollably. But ultimately, Clio silenced them with a keening that combined Hibernian lament with Levantine ululation. The crowd of pirates mulling about cackled their hearty approval.

While Horatio took his charges inside the Lafittes' shop, we continued on to *Le Pélican Nerveux*. Once more, the signage did much to explain the name. A group of pirates surrounded the worried bird while their captain gave it a randy wink. The scene appeared the prologue to that depicted at *Le Pélican Stupéfait*.

Avarice had prepped me well (verbally, I mean) in regard to Smedley's mannerisms and habits. He was, according to her, an arrogant bastard when it came to dealing with business associates.

"The manager is a woman," she told me.

"Like Clarisse?"

"You know Clarisse?"

"We met briefly. At the time, she must have assumed I was Smedley—she said something about having seen me only a week before."

"Excellent. Well, Hildegarde isn't quite so congenial as Clarisse. She's a good deal more... Viking-ish."

An odd adjective, I thought. But when she nodded toward a giantess off our starboard bow, I saw it was an apt one: about seven feet tall; blonde, nearly white hair; clear blue eyes; arms like a longshoreman's; and a vocabulary to match. She expressed this last in a patois combining French, English, and Swedish, but her forthright elocution—involving as it did a fair quantity of spittle—made it difficult to mistake her feelings. Contempt seemed preeminent among them.

I treated her in a like manner. And having learned my bullying at Annapolis, I was more than a match for the Norsewoman. We shouted at each other through frothing mouths, all quite disgusting, but it's the only way to communicate with some people, Vikings in particular. It took some time before I recognized her as Mrs. Erickson's twin. She was at least a foot taller, and an order of magnitude more vulgar, but otherwise the spitting image.

By then, Melpomene had taken the stage and begun singing sad French love songs. I wouldn't have thought pirates and their consorts were susceptible to such fare, but soon there wasn't a dry eye in the house. Even Hildegarde seemed affected. She'd given Avarice the books and the month's take was piled on the table in three even stacks. The first, she was to keep for operations; the second was her cut; and the third—the profits—we were to take. In counting, Avarice had managed to shave a fair amount from the first two stacks. But when Melpomene interposed a song with lyrics a tad too optimistic, the blonde giantess grew bored and became more attentive toward her loot.

I went over and coaxed my tireless tragedian off the stage by telling her she needed to rest her voice for the second set. Her half-sister, Pride, eagerly went on in her stead, twirling the end of her robe seductively as she entered the limelight. She'd been coached by Dottie, who claimed to have plied the pirate-haven burlesque circuit in her youth. For a moment, I feared the long-legged Sin might take things too fast. But she knew exactly what she was doing.

With the crowd now in her thrall, she gradually stilled the twirling, then broke into a thoroughly unique rendition of *Hookshop Kate,* the bawdy ballad of an insatiable *fille de joie* who sought her fortune first in the Klondike, then on the islands of Hawaii. The salty-tongued redhead took the tempo down to nothing, but made up for it with a sultry delivery that warmed the assembly's collective cockles. As if that weren't enough, at the end of each verse she'd do a slow pirouette and unravel another yard or two of robe. Quite arresting. But by working from the bottom up, she too soon revealed the feature buccaneers find most alluring.

During the ensuing pandemonium, Avarice made for the door with the loot and I went to retrieve her sisters. Luckily, Melpomene had dropped the curtain at the first sign of riot and she and Pride had managed to make it backstage. It took longer than expected to reach our alley rendezvous, and I was pleasantly surprised to find Avarice waiting.

"I'm touched. I thought for sure you'd leave with the

take," I made the mistake of telling her.

"*Don't be a simpleton!* I've got plans, that's all. Don't you see? We can pull the same thing in Barataria... and Tortuga. *Now quit wasting time!*"

In lauding a Mortal Sin, it's always important to remember who you're speaking with.

She handed me one of two cutlasses she'd somehow hidden in her robes, then led the way to the auction house. We arrived in time to witness a pirate's ejection from an upstairs window. On landing, he rose to his feet, looked back briefly—then fled the scene at breakneck speed.

"I suspect someone's upset Wrath," her sister said.

We went in to find Horatio and the auction clerk cowering behind the display cases, while Clio stood off to the side examining a shelf of books.

"You might want to make your exit about now," I told the clerk.

Being like-armed, he seemed unimpressed by my cutlass—but one look at Avarice's determined expression and he made for the street.

"Why are you down here?" I asked Horatio.

"Well, things got a little dangerous up there."

"We're wasting time! Come on!" Avarice shouted.

Horatio and I followed her upstairs. There we found three of Lafitte's men. All dead—but only one, as yet, filleted. Wrath, covered in blood and wielding a dagger, was making toward corpse number two.

I found poor Sesbania cowering in a corner while Envy badgered her. "Look at you! Why any man who'd had me would go after a waif like you is a complete mystery!"

Fortunately, Pride distracted the covetous Sin when

she appeared wearing a diamond tiara with matching necklace and earrings.

"Where'd you get that?"

The two of them scampered downstairs, as did their sisters—once Avarice managed to persuade Wrath her point had been amply made.

"Oh, Pluribus! I knew you'd come! But who are those strange women? And what did she mean by saying you'd *had* her?"

"Ah, well, it's a long, complicated story. But that can wait until we get back to the ship." And then some, I hoped.

"All right. But there is one thing.... Just to be sure...."

"What?"

She knelt down and pulled up my left trouser leg.

"Good. The scar. I just wanted to make sure. You may not believe it, but several times since the kidnapping, I've met people I know, who aren't them! They look, and sound, just like before. But they have different names, and have no idea who I am. I was worried you could be one of them...."

She swooned and I picked her up. Judging from her waistline, I thought it unlikely she still had the fifteen thousand in assorted currency strapped about her. Of course, if they'd had her on a starvation diet, there was still some chance....

II

The sun had risen by the time we returned to the ship, and we made way immediately. In the galley, Mattie had a terrapin soup waiting. Sesbania gulped down three bowls—then fell asleep at the table. After carrying her into my cabin, I assembled my harem.

"She's in a pretty delicate state. It might be best if we held off telling her about our arrangement just yet."

"Which arrangement?"

"Well, the polygamy."

"Does that include your tongue work?" Envy asked.

"Yes, that too."

"Not really worth mentioning," Avarice observed.

They all found that pretty amusing. All except Melpomene. Her eyes welled up, as they were wont to do, and she broke into a mournful tune about men's infidelity, and the suffering their women must endure because of it....

"Oh, for Christ's sake," Wrath interjected. "*Shut up!*"

She was the least talkative of all of them, but when she did speak, her sisters generally listened to her advice. A laudable trait, as was her attitude toward the parrot. She seemed to despise the creature with an even greater passion than I did. What's more, she could hit it with a sandal at forty paces—which she proved just then when it echoed Melpomene's most recent lament.

As I made to leave the familial confab, Avarice stopped me.

"We need to set course for Barataria and *Le Pélican Stupéfait*."

"This might not be the best time. Lafitte won't be happy when he sees what happened to his auction house. And his wares. Maybe we could give Barataria a pass?"

"No! Father always makes his rounds counterclockwise; we must do likewise, and strike before he realizes what we're up to." She interrupted herself to cackle. And she wasn't at all bad at it. Of course, she *was* a pirate's daughter. "I wish I could see his face when he discovers what we've done! He'll be furious!"

"Then perhaps it's best—"

"He'll be even more furious when he goes by the auction house and sees what I did to that book he lusted after," Clio interrupted.

"What book?"

"Shakespeare's *Titus Andronicus*. Only the second copy to have been found of the first quarto edition.... God, how I hate that play! I tore it into shreds, then peed on it!"

"Good girl! That will drive him mad!" Wrath told her.

Given he himself had already confirmed his condition in that regard, I found their blithe attitude rather disturbing. We would shortly have two very angry pirates after us, both of doubtful sanity, and both with ships far more powerful than ours. Even mild-tempered Jack was likely to be pretty annoyed with me for having abandoned him.

I pointed this out to Avarice, but she insisted that made it all the less likely they'd be expecting us to take the offensive. Admittedly, there was some truth in that. Plus, I badly needed to replenish the family funds. (While putting her to bed, I'd had occasion to ascertain that Sesbania had lost ours—not that I blamed her, exactly.)

I set us on a southwest course without mentioning to any of the others our ultimate destination. I suspected they'd object. And by then, I was thoroughly exhausted, and hardly in the mood for a mutiny. I went into my cabin and nestled up beside Sesbania. She made a little moan of contentment; soon we were both fast asleep.

I awoke to her stroking my hair.

"Let's get married," she said. "I mean, really married."

"I'm all for it.... But there are complicating factors...."

"*What* complicating factors?"

"Well... for one, if we were to get married here, would it be real? I mean, would it count when we get back?"

"Of course it would! Don't be an ass. What other complicating factors are there?"

I could think of seven offhand, but I didn't think it the ideal time to enumerate them.

"Well, for another thing, I'm broke.... By the way, I don't suppose you were able to keep their hands off that cache hidden beneath your garb?"

"Oh, they didn't lay a hand on me. My cache, as you call it, was never in danger. From what I could gather, the Lafittes' interest in women is purely financial."

"Well, that's a relief. But I meant the cache of currency you'd sewn into your lingerie."

"I... I don't remember that. In fact, I don't remember anything previous to the kidnapping aboard the *Paris*."

"You remembered my scar."

"Yes. I remember you, but little else. And thank you for shaving off that mustache. When I saw you yesterday, I thought I might be forced to get used to it."

"No, my barber felt the same way about it. Anyway, we can forget the money. You're here, and that's all that matters."

"Yes, that's all that matters.... But you *are* right, some money would be nice.... We don't need a fortune—at least, not right away.... Say, a few thousand, in a sound currency.... Or gilt-edged securities...."

Her display of wholehearted trust had left me feeling rather small. Until that moment, I'd still harbored some suspicion she might be a fictional double. Yes, even after she'd recognized me at the auction house, and shown she knew about my scar. And even after she revealed we'd never actually been married—not to mention her feelings regarding facial hair.

What finally cinched it was her concern for the negotiability of assets. Early on in our acquaintance, she'd demonstrated an unerring expertise in the area. It was one of several qualities that first won me over. She could spot a counterfeit banknote from across the room, and discern an underfunded bond issue by the smell of its ink. Her father had been a Washington lawyer and taught her well. Too well, I sometimes thought. One night, not long after we began traveling together, she recalled their last conversation:

"I won't ever forget what he told me that final evening we were together—ever!"

She was crying.

"What did he say?"

"He said, 'Promise me, Sesbania....'" She began sobbing uncontrollably. Only when she had finally composed herself did she continue. "He said, 'Promise me, Sesbania. Promise me that you'll never invest in a railroad.' And I did promise him!"

She's one of kind, all right. And not the type to test me the way I had her. Which was probably a good thing. You see, I've never been terribly attentive to details. For instance, that mole on her bum. If you'd asked me the day before, I'd have guessed it was on the left cheek....

The End ...more or less...

For those curious as to the resolution of the mole/bum conundrum, not to mention the proclivities of those Mortal Sins yet to be explored, our story, believe it or not, continues....

Them Shes Be Pirates, the second book of the Empyreal Privateer series, is available online and at all finer bookstores.

A Short Note on the Book's Authorship

The attentive reader will note two names on the title page of this work. The narrative is, primarily, the work of the tale's protagonist, E. Pluribus Van Slyke, and all credit, or blame, for the book's crude composition, rudimentary diction, and too frequent, overly graphic episodes of unseemly behavior may be laid at his benighted door. Likewise his numerous mischaracterizations of others—particularly members of his own extended family.

Nonetheless, the world he inhabits during the final three-fifths of the book is, both morally and ethically—if not precisely legally—the property of its orchestrator, M.E. Meegs.

And M.E. Meegs will certainly *not* be shortchanged.